FRASER VALLEY REGIONAL LIBRARY

39083500697066

ELLEN FRI

JOURNALIST

D0379865

# ELLEN FREMEDON, JOURNALIST

by

## Joan Givner

GROUNDWOOD BOOKS
HOUSE OF ANANSI PRESS
TORONTO   BERKELEY

Copyright © 2005 by Joan Givner

No part of this publication may be reproduced, stored in a retrieval system or transmitted, in any form or by any means, without the prior written consent of the publisher or a licence from The Canadian Copyright Licensing Agency (Access Copyright). For an Access Copyright licence, visit www.accesscopyright.ca or call toll free to 1-800-893-5777.

Groundwood Books / House of Anansi Press
110 Spadina Avenue, Suite 801, Toronto, Ontario M5V 2K4

Distributed in the USA by Publishers Group West
1700 Fourth Street, Berkeley, CA 94710

We acknowledge for their financial support of our publishing program the Canada Council for the Arts, the Government of Canada through the Book Publishing Industry Development Program (BPIDP) and the Ontario Arts Council.

ONTARIO ARTS COUNCIL
CONSEIL DES ARTS DE L'ONTARIO

Library and Archives Canada Cataloguing in Publication

Givner, Joan.
Ellen Fremedon: journalist / by Joan Givner
ISBN-13: 978-0-88899-668-8 (bound).–
ISBN-10: 0-88899-668-3 (bound).–
ISBN-13: 978-0-88899-691-6 (pbk.) –
ISBN-10: 0-88899-691-8 (pbk.)
I. Title.
PS 8563.I86E453 2005    jC813'.54    C2005-902919-6

Cover illustration by Rebecca Buchanan
Design by Michael Solomon
Printed in Canada

*This story about two loyal friends*
*is dedicated to*
*LeeAnne Schienbein,*
*and to the memory of*
*Emily Givner*

# CONTENTS

| | | |
|---|---|---|
| 1 | Summer Plans | 9 |
| 2 | Mrs. T. | 17 |
| 3 | A Mysterious Stranger | 28 |
| 4 | The Partridge Inquirer | 36 |
| 5 | Investigative Reporting | 46 |
| 6 | Mistakes | 53 |
| 7 | A Meeting | 59 |
| 8 | A Visit | 67 |
| 9 | Next Issue | 75 |
| 10 | Paparazzi | 82 |
| 11 | Interviewing Higg | 91 |
| 12 | A Shock | 97 |
| 13 | Confidences | 106 |
| 14 | Conversations | 116 |
| 15 | An Editorial | 125 |
| 16 | Revelations | 131 |
| 17 | Calm Weather | 139 |
| 18 | Final Interview | 146 |
| 19 | More Revelations | 154 |
| 20 | Fame | 161 |
| 21 | Endings | 169 |

# 1
# SUMMER PLANS

WHEN I THINK ABOUT the strange things that happened this past summer, it seems they began when two newcomers came to Partridge Cove. What was weird was that the new people came around the same time, although they arrived in different ways.

The first one slipped into the neighborhood very quietly, and we first noticed she was there the day my friend Jenny and I decided to put out our newspaper.

It was the first day of the summer holidays. Jenny and I were at the bottom of our garden in the little house that Mum and Dad gave me. It used to be a tool shed, but we cleaned it up and painted it. Jenny named it Something Cottage — Somecot for short.

Jenny was sitting at my desk with a pile of colored paper squares and a library book propped up in front of her. It was called *Japanese Origami.*

Origami was her latest hobby. It means making things by folding paper. She wasn't very good at it yet, but Jenny never gives up once she's started something. For most of the afternoon she'd been trying to make animals and birds, but so far there was just a lot of scrunched-up paper on the floor around her. It looked the way the floor looks when somebody's in bed with a cold and keeps throwing tissues on the floor. Only these were all different colors.

I was lying on the floor, not doing anything. I was thinking that we'd looked forward to school being out for weeks, and now the whole summer stretched ahead like a big nothing. I couldn't think of a single thing I wanted to do.

"Last summer was so much fun," I said.

"You didn't think so at the time," Jenny said.

That was true. Parts of last summer were horrible. The water supply in Partridge Cove was threatened by a developer who planned to build four hundred houses over in Lodgepole Meadows. We tried to stop the building, discovered we had a secret enemy, and the twins disappeared. I put it all in a book I wrote.

"I thought you were going to write another book," Jenny said.

"There's no point writing books," I said. "Nobody wants to buy books when they can get them free from the library. It's just a lot of hard work."

"Can you tell me what this is?" Jenny said, holding up the paper she'd been folding.

"A kite?"

"It's supposed to be a swan," she said. "I'll have to do better than this if I'm going to enter something in the arts and crafts competition at the Cobble Hill Fair."

For a while neither of us said anything. I was thinking about the Cobble Hill Fair. There were competitions for art and growing flowers and raising pets and writing poetry and reciting poetry, but there was no competition for writing a book.

"Can you tell what this is?" she said, holding up a folded paper in bright orange. It looked like another kite.

"A swan?" I said.

"It's supposed to be a goldfish."

"Why don't you draw some scales and an eye on it, to make it look more like a fish?" I said, trying to sound encouraging.

"If you want to write something that makes

money," Jenny said, "why don't you write a news-paper? Everybody buys newspapers."

"That's not a bad idea."

"Well, it was your own idea. Don't you remem-ber how all the papers had a lot of rude stuff about your family in them after the twins disappeared?"

"Sure," I said. "It was all lies."

"And how you said you'd like to put out your own paper with true things in it instead of a lot of rumors?"

"Hm."

"If you did that," Jenny said, "you could sell it. Even people who never read books read newspa-pers."

"You're right," I said. "Mr. Floyd usually has a paper spread out on the counter when you go into the Clothes Loft to buy something. He reads the sports section."

"I always look for the cartoons," Jenny said.

"Mum does the crossword puzzles."

"My mom cuts out recipes."

"Dad writes letters to the editor when he sees something in the paper that isn't true or doesn't make sense."

"Running a newspaper would get you a lot more money than writing a book," Jenny said. "I could help you with it, and we could split the money. A newspaper isn't like a book. A lot of different people can work on it."

"That's true."

"You could be the editor and I could be the business manager," she said.

"You could draw the pictures, too. Newspapers have a lot of pictures in them."

Just then the ship's bell on the deck up at the house rang several times, which meant it was time for me to help with the next meal. So Jenny packed up her stuff and we hurried up the garden and into the kitchen.

"Hi, there, you two," Dad said. "Sorry to drag you up from Somecot but I could use some help with the scalloped potatoes. The potatoes need peeling, and I can't seem to find the cheese in the fridge."

So we got to work. I started in on the potatoes, and Jenny looked for the cheese. Mum's illness had got worse since last summer and the twins were too young to help much, so Dad and I were doing all the cooking.

Jenny stayed for supper, but the food wasn't very good. There weren't enough onions in the scalloped potatoes, and we used Cheez Whiz because we'd run out of real cheese. Meals were going downhill pretty fast.

We first noticed that something unusual was going on in the house next door when we were in the middle of a discussion about what to call our paper.

"A lot of papers are called *The Sun* or *The Star*," I said.

"Why are they never called *The Moon*?" Jenny said. "We could call our paper *The Moonbeam*, or *The Moonstone*."

"Some important papers are called *The Times*," Dad said. "There's *The Times* in England. Then there's the *New York Times* in the United States. Its motto is 'All the news that's fit to print.'"

"That would be a good motto for our paper," I said.

"You could call it *Somecot Times*," Mum said, "because that's where your editorial office will be."

"*The Observer*, *The Leader Post*, *The Plain-Dealer*, *The Village Voice*, *The Inquirer*…" Dad was listing the names of all the newspapers he could think of when he suddenly stopped, got up and went over to the window.

"That's odd," he said. "There are lights on in Satis Lodge."

Satis Lodge is the house next door. It was empty for years, the garden got all wild and tangled, and it was our favorite place to play. Then a year ago, some horrible people we called the Maggots moved in. They cut down all the trees, made a concrete patio and completely wrecked the place. Then they went away, leaving it bare and ugly.

We all joined Dad at the window, looking over the hedge at the lights in the windows of Satis Lodge.

"Do you suppose there's someone inside who has no right to be there?" Dad said.

He was thinking of all the vandalism that had been taking place recently in Partridge Cove. Fires had been set in garbage cans, street signs had been torn down, and mail boxes had been pushed over.

"Maybe it's a den of thieves," the twins said.

"I think you'd better give Cathy Banks a call," Mum said. Cathy Banks is an RCMP officer, and she knows about everything and everybody in Partridge Cove. So Dad went into his study and made a phone call.

When he came back to the table, he said that Satis Lodge had been rented for the summer by a woman and her companion. Nobody knew where they came from or why they were there. All the arrangements had been made through the real estate office in the village by an agency in the United States.

In a small village like ours, there's always a lot of

excitement when someone new appears on the scene. If a big yacht appears in the inlet, people get out their binoculars and try to spot famous movie stars on the deck. So naturally we all started talking about the new woman and her companion. I didn't have any great hopes myself since the last neighbors were such a disaster.

Anyway, all this made us forget about naming our paper for a while. By the time we remembered what we'd been talking about, it was getting late, so I decided to make a list of all the names everyone had suggested. Then Jenny closed her eyes, took her fork and stabbed at the list. It landed between *The Village Voice* and *The Inquirer*, so we decided to call our paper *The Partridge Cove Inquirer*.

We didn't realize at the time what a good name it was, and how many bizarre events there would be for us to inquire into before the summer was over.

# 2
# MRS. T.

THERE WAS NOTHING QUIET about the way Mrs. T. arrived. She turned up the night after we'd decided to put out a newspaper.

Dad had put an ad on the notice board in the village for two positions. One was for a housekeeper for a family with three young children. The other was for a nurse/caregiver for an invalid, because that's what Mum was now, and she could no longer do much in the house or the garden. The first person who called about a job took one look at the mess in the living room, and at us, and said we needed someone younger. Another one took the housekeeping job, but the morning she started work, there were two mice running around the house. The twins had bought them because they wanted to start a petting zoo, but they didn't have enough money for a cage. The woman said, "I don't want to work in no zoo," and left. After that, we managed the best we could.

We'd almost given up hope when Mrs. T. showed up. We were in the middle of supper when the doorbell rang. Dad opened the door, and a tall thin woman was standing on the step.

"Mrs. T. Housekeeper," she said.

She hadn't called ahead, but Dad said she'd better join us at the table, and he introduced us.

"This is my daughter, Ellen," he said, "and the twins are Timmy and Toby."

I quickly set an extra place, feeling that we wouldn't make a good impression. There were no mice because Dad had made the twins take them back to the pet shop, but I hadn't cleared the lunch things away before I made supper and the kitchen was full of dirty dishes. We were having chili, and Dad offered her some. She asked for just a bit, sniffed at it, and ate a small spoonful as if she was afraid she might get poisoned.

"We ran out of tomato sauce so I used tomato soup instead," I said. "And I used green beans instead of kidney beans."

It looked worse than it tasted, though it didn't actually taste very good, either.

Then Dad asked if Mrs. T. had found us through the ad on the notice board.

"I don't read the notice board," she said. "I heard about the job, and I felt the call to serve."

"Which position?" Dad asked.

"Both."

"Both?" Dad said. "Oh, I think that will be far too much work for one person."

"I'm used to hard labor," she said. "As a preacher's wife, I had to be." Dad asked her if she was used to children. She said she and the Reverend hadn't been blessed with children of their own, but they'd fostered a bunch. And when the Lord called the Reverend to his side, she'd been left to raise them on her own.

"What's fostered?" asked Toby, going a bit pale.

"The Reverend and I took them in because they didn't have any parents, or if they did, they weren't able to raise them," she said.

"Why weren't they able to raise them?" Tim said.

"Because!" she said. We waited to hear more but that seemed to be all Mrs. T. was going to say on the subject.

"If everyone's finished, perhaps you and I should have a talk about references, the duties involved, and the salary," Dad said.

"Looks to me like the first order of duty should

be that sink full of dirty dishes," Mrs T. said. "You kids carry in your plates, and Ellen and I will see to them."

"Very well," said Dad, picking up his plate and heading toward the kitchen.

"The kitchen's no place for a man," Mrs. T. said, blocking his way. "Ellen and I will do them." She washed the dishes and told me to dry them and put them away. While we worked, she asked me a lot of questions about mealtimes and shopping, and what we had for breakfast. When we'd almost finished, Dad came out of his study to talk to her.

"It's too late for talking now," she said. "My hours are eight to five, but I'll get here earlier tomorrow, as it's my first day."

"May I drive you somewhere?" Dad asked.

"I'll make my own way home," she said. "I need to pick up some things at the store." And she headed down the road in the direction of the village.

"Did you hire her?" I asked Dad.

"I'm not sure," he said.

The next day she arrived early, and she was carrying a bag full of groceries. She made soup for lunch from the stuff she'd brought in the bag. It simmered on top of the stove all morning and filled the house with an amazing smell so we couldn't wait to eat it. We had huge appetites by lunch time.

Even Mum came to the table in her wheelchair. Mrs. T. served us all and sat down. Then she looked at Dad as if she expected him to do something.

"Shall we bow our heads in prayer?" she said.

He swallowed for a moment and looked around the table. Mum had a little smile on her face. We all waited to see what he would say. Finally he put his spoon down.

"No," he said. "We shall not bow our heads in prayer."

"Do you object to thanking the Good Lord for the bounty he provides?" Mrs. T. said.

"In the first place, we don't accept the Good Lord as the provider of this bounty," Dad said.

"Do you mean to tell me you're raising these children without religion?" she said. "How do you expect them to know right from wrong?"

"Knowing the difference between right and wrong is never easy," Dad said, "and I don't believe religion increases our ability to do it. Quite the contrary. But I must ask you to respect our beliefs, as we shall respect yours. If you wish to say grace, please do so before this excellent soup gets cold."

Gran usually says, "Lord, bless this food to our use and us to thy service," but Mrs. T. seemed to be on more friendly terms with the Lord. She closed her eyes, bowed her head and started having a long conversation with him. She thanked him for leading her to a house where she was sorely needed, and she asked him to give her strength for the difficult task ahead. Then she asked him to look down on those who walk in darkness and help them to see the light. Finally she thanked him for his many blessings, especially for blessing us with the food for this good meal.

Even the twins just watched in amazement, until she opened her eyes and looked around the table, as if she expected us to clap or say something. Mum said, "Amen," and we all picked up our spoons.

Mrs. T. was quite right about the meal being good. The soup had carrots and ginger in it, and everything she made after that was delicious.

"This is the best soup I ever put in my mouth," Tim said.

Dad said he couldn't believe how the food bill had dropped since Mrs. T. came. She more than made up for the amount he paid her. Mum hadn't had much of an appetite, but now it picked up. She's a vegetarian and doesn't eat anything that has a face. The food Mrs. T. cooked had a lot of vegetables in it, and Mum ate everything. Mrs. T. went straight to the kitchen when she arrived in the morning and got the food started. Then she helped Mum with her bath and got her settled for the day.

The worst part about having Mrs. T. in charge was that we had porridge for breakfast. She taught me how to make it the first day, and then told me it would be my job to get the porridge started every morning before she got here.

"My grandmother used to make porridge," Dad said.

"It's like the three bears," I said.

"Will there be porridge for breakfast for the rest of our lives?" Toby said.

"On Saturday, there'll be pancakes," said Mrs. T., "for boys who've eaten all their porridge on week-days."

"I don't like being blessed with porridge," Timmy said. "I won't eat it unless you put choco-late on it." He's very fussy about food. He calls tapi-oca pudding frogs' eggs, but he'll eat it if Dad grates some chocolate on it.

"No chocolate on porridge," Mrs. T. said. But she put a spoonful of her homemade jam on the twins' porridge, and they both ate it.

"Why do you say grace before the meal instead of after?" said Timmy. "What if you aren't thankful for it because it's awful, like Ellen's chili?"

"There are plenty of children in the world who would be glad to eat Ellen's chili, or get any food at all," Mrs. T. said.

"Well, why doesn't the Lord give them more food?" Timmy said. "Is he trying to teach them a lesson?"

"When I was your age," Mrs T. said, "children were seen and not heard."

"If they weren't heard, how could they ask questions?" Timmy said. "And if they couldn't ask questions, they must have grown up stupid."

"That's enough out of you," Mrs. T. said.

We were gradually getting used to Mrs. T.'s ways. She was very bossy and strict, and she made a lot of rules about washing our hands before we ate, and not leaving any food on our plates. We were all a bit scared of her, even Dad.

"Professor," she said, when he left his coat lying on the sofa, "how can we expect these children to be neat and tidy when you set a bad example by leaving your clothes all over the place."

"Quite right, Mrs. T.," he said, picking up his coat and putting it on a coat hanger, but he wouldn't let her in his study to clean it.

She stayed all day. By late afternoon she'd made most of the preparations for dinner, and all I had to do was put things in the oven and serve them up.

"I want to say grace," Timmy said one day as we sat down to supper. We all looked at Dad to see what he would say, but he just ignored Timmy and started eating. Timmy closed his eyes tight and put his hands together.

"O Lord," he said, "I hate porridge. I hate having it every morning. It's an abomination and it sucks. Thanks for the food, but stop giving us porridge, or I might run away and live on a desert island." (Dad was reading the twins *Robinson Crusoe* at night.)

"I don't think you're supposed to threaten the Lord," Toby said.

But the funny thing was, his prayer seemed to work.

"Ellen, it's getting too hot to cook porridge," Mrs. T. said the next morning. "We'll switch to cold cereal and fruit for breakfast." So for the rest of the summer we had granola and sliced bananas.

Timmy said that proved the Lord had heard him.

"I think that was a coincidence rather than a cause," Dad said.

"That's a fallacy," I said. "Post hoc ergo propter hoc."

"Mrs. T. says the Lord listens to the weakest of his children when they humbly ask for his help," Toby said.

"He didn't ask humbly," I said. "He asked rudely."

"I'm not the weakest," Timmy said. "I can do a lot of things better than you guys."

"Yeah, like what?" I said.

"Like whatever!"

Timmy kept saying grace and asking for things he wanted to eat. Instead of the granola from the bulk food section of the supermarket that we now had every day, he wanted Cheerios and Frosted Flakes in boxes, and packets of cereal with surprises and presents inside.

None of these prayers was answered.

"The Lord doesn't heed the wishes of every small boy who doesn't appreciate the blessings he has," Mrs. T. said when Timmy complained.

At lunch the next day, Mrs. T. closed her eyes and put her hands together, and we all waited for her to start talking to God. She didn't, and after a while she opened her eyes again and said, "Is that basket of bread stuck to the table?" When we looked surprised, she told us she'd said grace silently. After that, she always said grace silently. I thought she'd got fed up with us listening to her private conversations with the Lord, or maybe she was telling him things about us walking in darkness that she didn't want us to hear.

"I think, on the whole, the Good Lord did very

well in sending Mrs. T. to help us out," Dad said one day when he and I were clearing up after supper.

"Dad!" I said.

"That's just a manner of speaking," he said.

# 3
# A MYSTERIOUS
# STRANGER

"WE'VE BEEN BLESSED WITH a new housekeeper," Tim said when Gran came up for Sunday lunch.

"And how is she working out?"

"She gave me a night-light to put by my bed."

Tim got the night-light after Mrs. T. asked me why the twins were allowed to leave their light on all night. I told her that Tim had been scared of the dark ever since he got shut in a shed last summer, and so after that Dad had let them leave their light on.

The next day Mrs. T. produced the night-light out of her bag, and Tim liked it a lot. When the light's on, it looks as if fish are swimming round and round. Dad said it must have been expensive, but no doubt it would be worth it in the long run because it would save on the electric bill. I said I'd seen one just like it in the gift shop, and it cost twenty dollars. Mrs. T. said she hadn't paid twenty dollars. It had a small chip on the rim that you could hardly see, so because it was flawed, it cost hardly anything.

Whenever we needed some utensil or appliance, like a slotted spoon or a Pyrex dish, Mrs. T. brought one in the next day.

"It's amazing how Mrs. T. is able to find things at garage sales and church fairs that have hardly been used," Dad told Gran. "Since she arrived, we've acquired a blender, an electric can-opener, a rice cooker and a handy little gadget for grating cheese. She picks them up for a song and they're like new."

"I think people buy these new-fangled appliances and then find it's quicker to do things by hand than to have to clean them and find a place to store them," Gran said. "I've never been a believer in electrical appliances myself."

"You use a washing machine and a dryer, don't you?" Mum said.

"I do use a washing machine, but I don't like using a dryer," Gran said. "My laundry never smells as sweet as it did when I hung it out in the fresh air to dry. I read recently that the Queen insists on having her sheets dried in the open air."

"Oh, yes, I've noticed all the clotheslines up around Buckingham Palace," Mum said. "They hang out the wash between the changing of the guard and one of their garden parties."

"I think Gran might like another helping of these excellent vegetables," Dad said quickly. "We have Mrs. T. to thank for them, too."

"The Good Lord puts his bounty in Mrs. T.'s garden," Tim said, "and we get to eat it."

"Apparently she has a green thumb and grows more vegetables than one person can eat," Dad said. "So she kindly brings the surplus to us."

"We've been blessed with new neighbors, too," Tim said.

"More friendly than the last ones, I trust," Gran said.

"Our new neighbors keep to themselves," Dad said. "We know very little about them. Though, of course, the rumor mill is busy as always."

"I make it a rule to ignore neighborhood gossip," Gran said.

"That's very high-minded of you, Mother," Dad said. "I'm afraid the rest of us have been indulging our curiosity."

"And what have you found out?"

"We think one lady's hiding from the police," Toby said.

"Good gracious! Whatever has she done?"

"We think she murdered someone, and there's a humongous reward for her capture. But we won't get it because we aren't allowed over there," Timmy said.

"What makes you think such dreadful things?" Gran said.

"It's logical," Toby said. "She's in disguise. People in disguise have something to hide. Therefore she's done something she wants to hide."

"The twins have a faulty premise there," Dad said. "Dark glasses and a large hat do not necessarily constitute a disguise."

"She probably wants to protect her eyes and skin," Mum said. "I'm always telling you children not to go out into the sun without hats, but you never listen."

"They come from another country," Toby said. "The old woman doesn't speak English."

"Who says she doesn't speak English?" Dad said.

"Mr. Weeks stood next to her at the checkout counter," Toby said.

"Mr. Weeks is practically deaf," I said, "and he

won't wear a hearing aid. He tells everybody they're mumbling or talking Double Dutch."

"Well, it is weird that the younger woman never leaves the house or walks to the village like everyone else," Toby said. "And the only visitor is a man who comes every Wednesday in a big car."

"Perhaps she's come here to convalesce from an illness in a quiet place by the sea," Mum said. "I expect the old woman is a nurse or caregiver who's looking after her."

But Jenny thought she might have come to Partridge Cove to recover from a broken heart. We talked about it one day when she was having supper with us. Jenny only comes to the house now after Mrs. T.'s gone home. One of the bad things about Mrs. T. is that she can't stand having Jenny around because Jenny's mother and Cathy Banks live together. Mrs. T. disapproves of women living together as partners. She says it's a sin and an abomination. Some of the kids at school say the same thing, so Jenny is used to it, but it still hurts her feelings.

"Maybe the young woman will meet someone here," I said, "and then they'll get married and have a family, and there'll be kids and ponies around the house."

"She won't meet anyone if she never goes out,"

Jenny said. "And besides, there isn't anyone in the village for her to marry."

"There's Larry at the library," I said.

"But he's short and fat."

"That doesn't necessarily disqualify a person from getting married," Mum said.

"No," said Dad, "even I managed to persuade someone to marry me, in spite of my unprepossessing appearance."

"But you had lots of hair when Mum married you," Timmy said.

"That's true," Dad said, "but I think Mum was looking for other qualities, such as a kind heart."

"Well, Larry has a kind heart," I said.

"Maybe she'll leave a library book out in the rain," Jenny said, "and when she takes it back she'll discover how kind he is, and she'll fall madly in love with him."

"He isn't very kind when I leave a book out in the rain," Timmy said.

"That's because you do it all the time," I said. "He should have blessed you with a black eye."

"Ellen, please!" Dad said.

I asked if Jenny and I could be excused, so we took our dessert and ate it sitting on the steps outside Somecot. Mrs. T. had made a bread pudding with leftover bread and cream and lots of raisins. It was pretty good, and while we ate it we looked across at Satis Lodge.

That gave me an idea. I said it was a journalist's job to find out what was going on in the community, so I would try to investigate the new neighbors. If they were criminals, I didn't want the twins getting the reward for finding them instead of me.

"Well, you can't find out about them when the old woman won't talk to anyone, and the young woman never goes out," Jenny said.

"I could ask if they need help with the garden. Then as I work I could look for clues."

"But they don't need a gardener. They have the Green Thumb Landscaping Service. I've seen the van outside."

I had, too. Soon after the women arrived, the van drove up from the city. It was full of shrubs and trees in tubs. Men in green overalls carried them in and put them at the back of the house where the Maggots had cut down the trees the year before. The new plants weren't as big as the trees, but they made the place look a bit less bare. There were a lot of expensive flowering plants like oleanders and hibiscus and orange trees. They set them around the patio so that it was shady and cool. And each week after that, they came back to look after the garden.

"Gardening services just do big jobs like mowing the grass and weed-eating and pruning the trees," I said. "There are always a lot of little jobs they don't do, like weeding gravel paths and rockeries. That's where I come in."

Jenny said it wouldn't work, and that we should find other things to investigate, such as who was doing all the vandalism. I thought that was impossible because the vandals were probably people from the city who were just passing through. We get a lot of bikers in Partridge Cove during the summer months. They roar up and down the country lanes, sometimes in ones and twos and sometimes in gangs. They break the speed limit and make a lot of noise. Cathy says it's impossible to catch them, so I didn't see how I could investigate them.

I didn't want to get into an argument with Jenny just then, but I thought that after we got the first issue of our paper out in a day or two, I'd give the gardening idea a try.

# 4
# THE PARTRIDGE INQUIRER

THE FIRST ISSUE OF our newspaper looked beautiful. At the top of the front page Jenny had printed *The Partridge Inquirer* in big letters, all decorated with flowers and leaves, with partridges perching on the letters. She meant to write *The Partridge Cove Inquirer* but she was concentrating so hard on the birds that she accidentally left out *Cove.*

Underneath the paper's name she wrote *All the news that's fit to print* and our names:

ELLEN FREMEDON, EDITOR-IN-CHIEF
JENNY BROWN, BUSINESS MANAGER & ART DIRECTOR

I wrote an editorial explaining why we were

having a newspaper and what was special about it. I said we were going to tell our readers about all the activities going on in Partridge Cove during the summer. It would be a truthful account of what was happening with no lies or mistakes.

On the front page we had an article about a terrible thing that had just happened. Somebody had dumped a whole box of detergent in the artificial pond in front of the supermarket and had killed all the fish in there. It isn't a natural pond like the one in our garden, but it's still pretty. There's a little waterfall over some rocks, a lot of water lilies and marigolds, and it's full of different kinds of fish. People often sit on the benches beside it to rest while they're doing errands. So everyone was talking about it and wondering who could have done such a stupid thing.

We tried to interview the supermarket manager about the death of the fish, but he just said, "You two probably know more about it than I do." Then we interviewed Cathy Banks and she told us there was no word yet on who did it, but the investigation was ongoing. So we put that in the paper.

Newspapers usually have shocking headlines that attract attention and make people want to buy the paper, so we thought hard about the headline for this article. We considered *Terrorist Act at Fish*

*Pond*, *Crime Wave in Partridge Cove* and *Fish Murdered by Poison*.

Finally we settled for *A Senseless Act of Vandalism*. Underneath the headline Jenny drew a picture of a man wearing a black mask and a cloak, riding a motorcycle. He had a box of Sunshine Soap under one arm.

On the second page we had an obituary section. We interviewed two neighbors who had lost their pets. They both said they were very happy that their pets would have memorials and that that was a good thing about a small paper.

*ELVIS FENWICK, beloved parrot of Mr. and Mrs. Fenwick. On May 30th, of natural causes. Survived by owners Mr. and Mrs. Fenwick. Predeceased by Bing, Polly, Myrtle, Whiskers, Tiddlywinks, Peg and Bouncer. Elvis had a long, happy life, was very good at whistling, and could talk. He said, "Mind your own business," and "That's what you think."*

*ROVER BANKS, beloved dog of Mr. and Mrs. Banks. Rover went to the happy hunting grounds in April, age twelve. He was really Mr. Banks' dog, but it was Mrs. Banks who cried for two days after he passed away. Also sadly missed by Cathy Banks. Mr. and Mrs. Banks had Rover since he was a puppy. They got him from the humane society. Rover could sit up and beg and shake hands with visitors, and he was very friendly.*

It was Jenny's idea to say that Rover had gone to the happy hunting grounds. In actual fact, Mr. and Mrs. Banks had him put down.

Jenny also put a notice in the paper about her canary who died last summer.

### IN MEMORIAM

*SONATA BROWN, beloved canary of Jenny Brown. Suddenly, last July. Sonata came from a pet shop in Vancouver and had a very happy life. Sonata was a pretty shade of yellow, and a very talented singer.*

I was going to put "survived by Sebastian Brown," but Jenny said that her cat didn't deserve to get mentioned because he was the one who had eaten Sonata.

Besides the obituaries, we had a cooking section, and I put in my recipe for muffins.

## *ELLEN FREMEDON'S*
## *BLACKBERRY MUFFINS*

*1/2 cup butter*
*1/2 cup sugar*
*1 free-range brown egg*
*2 teaspoons baking powder*
*1 1/2 cups flour*
*1/2 cup milk*

*Blend the butter and sugar and then add the beaten egg. Put the baking powder in the flour and add some of it to the mixture. After you have added about half, start putting the milk in, then more flour and more milk until your mixture is nice and smooth.*

*Put paper cups in your muffin pans, and put a big spoonful of the mixture in each cup. Then make a circle of berries on top of it and put one in the middle. Then put another spoonful of mixture on top. This is better than mixing the berries into the dough because the soft berries are easily squished.*

*Before you start, put the oven on at 350 degrees. When you put the muffin tray in the oven, set the timer for 35 minutes. If they are not done at the end of 35 minutes, keep look-*

*ing at them until they are brown. Then take*
*them out and eat them right away.*

We thought our newspaper was really good
value for the money. Jenny had worked out the
prices. Each copy cost fifty cents. At first we
thought we might put out a copy each week, but
Mum said that might be too much pressure, so we
decided on a bi-weekly paper. That meant we
would get out two issues a month, so if anyone
wanted to take a monthly subscription, they could
pay a dollar. If they wanted a subscription for three
months, they could pay three dollars.

We were surprised by how many people wanted subscriptions for three months. Gran bought
two three-month subscriptions, and Mrs. Banks
bought two. We ran into Mr. Higginson in the village. He was our teacher last year and we liked him
a lot. He thought the newspaper was an excellent
idea, and he bought a three-month subscription,
too.

Soon we had sold twenty-five subscriptions,
and we had seventy-five dollars. We opened a bank
account at Partridge Cove Savings and put the
money in it. We had seventy-eight dollars by then
because we also sold a subscription to the teller
who set up our bank account. Jenny said not all the

money was clear profit because there were a lot of expenses involved in putting out a newspaper. The main expenses were for paper, notebooks, pencils, and putting money in the photocopying machine at the library.

We were so pleased with our first issue that we decided to celebrate. I suggested we go to Mrs. A.'s Candy Kitchen and get double-dip ice cream cones. Jenny said we do that all the time and we ought to do something more special. She said we should go to the Creamery for lunch.

It's really nice at the Creamery. There's a pile of newspapers, and they let you read them while you wait for your food. We chose a big table in the window so that we could spread the newspapers out. When Tracy brought our menus, she said the specials of the day were clam chowder and an egg salad sandwich. I thought that sounded good, but Jenny said when you eat out you should order something you can't get at home, so she ordered a taco wrap and I ordered a quesadilla. We both ordered medium root beers.

While we waited, we looked through the papers for ideas. Some tell how many people buy the paper, so we decided to put "Circulation 26" on ours. One newspaper had an Arts section with book reviews, and an interview with a writer, and a big picture of the writer. Another had a column where people with problems could write letters asking for advice. They signed them Confused, Cheated, and Single Mom. At the top of the column was a picture of the woman who gave the advice.

I thought an advice column was a great idea. I suggested we call it "Aunt Partridge's Advice," and Jenny could draw a picture of Aunt Partridge. Jenny said she couldn't think of anyone who would write to us for advice. I said we could write the first letters ourselves, as well as answering them. Nobody would know we wrote them if we signed the letters Unhappy or Puzzled in Partridge Cove.

As we were eating lunch, people we knew stopped by our table to say hello. Pat and Myra from the bookstore said they had enjoyed our paper and couldn't wait to read the next issue. Larry came in by himself, so we invited him to sit with us.

"I appreciate the invitation," he said, "but I like a bit of peace and quiet after a morning in the library. Besides, you girls are probably having a working lunch, and making a lot of important editorial decisions." We told him that was true, and that we'd decided to put book reviews in our paper.

"Excellent idea," he said. "I'll let you know about the new books that come in."

Just then I happened to look out the window. A very ugly face was pressed against it, with the nose squished against the window pane, crawling up it like a snail. When it saw me looking, it put its thumb in its ears and wiggled its fingers.

It made me so mad to think I couldn't have lunch without being bothered by the twins. Toby wasn't so bad, but Timmy was becoming a serious pest.

"Ellen, you should tell those twins of yours not to hang around the restaurant," Tracy said. "It annoys the other customers."

"They're not my twins. They just happen to live at my house. Unfortunately."

"Just ignore him and he'll get tired of making faces," Jenny said.

"Would you like the dessert menu?" Tracy said. "We have a good selection of cheesecakes and pastries."

We ordered two pieces of carrot cake, and then we needed two more root beers to wash them down.

I thought we should eat lunch at the Creamery more often. I changed my mind, though, when Tracy brought the bill.

"Jenny, it's over thirty dollars," I said. "There must be a mistake."

"Let's see," Jenny said. "The wrap and the quesadilla were six dollars each, and the dessert was five dollars. It was the root beers that pushed it up. We had four at two-fifty each. Then there was tax on top of that."

We managed to scrape enough money together to pay the bill, but there wasn't enough for a tip. We explained to Tracy that the bill was a lot more than we'd expected, and we offered to give her a copy of our newspaper instead.

"Don't worry about it," she said.

"We're going to have to sell some more subscriptions," Jenny said.

"Everyone we know already has subscriptions."

"What about your new neighbor? Maybe you should investigate her after all. You could sell her a subscription at the same time."

# 5
# INVESTIGATIVE
# REPORTING

THE NEXT MORNING I went to the front door of Satis Lodge and rang the bell. I heard it ringing inside, and when no one came to the door, I rang it again and again.

I was just about to leave when the door suddenly flew open, and the old woman stood there glaring at me.

"What d'you want making that hullabaloo?"

"I see you have a lot of weeds in your path," I said, "and I wondered if you needed any help getting them out."

"How can you help?"

"I just dig them out with a knife," I said. "It's the best way. I charge two dollars an hour. I work for a lot of the neighbors. They'll give me a good reference if you call them."

"I want nothing to do with neighbors," the woman said.

Just then someone appeared in the shadows at the end of the hall.

"Who is it?" a woman's voice cried out. Then the old woman said something that I couldn't understand.

"Well, why not?" the voice said. "The garden does seem to need more attention than it's been getting." She had a funny accent but it wasn't French or English or American.

"When can you start?" the old woman said to me, and I told her I could come the next day.

I began with all the small jobs that the gardening services don't do. I weeded the gravel path, dead-headed all the petunias in a flowerbed, and all the roses, and I scraped the moss and stuff out of the cracks in a wall. When I'd finished, I went to the front door, and the old woman came out and looked at what I'd done. She just nodded and then she gave me my money. One of them must have spotted me when I arrived, because she gave me the right amount for the exact time I spent there.

No one asked me if I wanted a drink of water, or

said I could feel free to go inside if I needed to use the bathroom. I figured if no one ever spoke to me I wouldn't be able to do much investigating. The house was very quiet. I never heard the radio or television or phone ringing or talking.

The only time there was something to hear was on Wednesday when the man arrived in a car. He came in the morning, carried a cardboard box into the house, and left with another cardboard box in the late afternoon. It was a sunny day, and he and the younger woman sat on the patio chatting while they had something to eat and drink. I went to the part of the path near the house and started weeding there, so that I could listen to what they were saying. I couldn't hear everything because sometimes they rattled the cups and plates, or walked to the other side of the patio. But I did hear bits of conversation, and they were very interesting.

"Is it quiet enough for you here?" the man said.

"Oh, yes indeed," the woman said in her funny accent. "Quiet as the grave, except for the birdsong. And I can hear roosters in the morning."

"So this place suits you, then."

"It's very beautiful and peaceful," she said. "A person could have a good life here."

"It's an ideal climate," he said.

"I wasn't thinking of the weather," she said. "I feel safe here."

"For the moment," he said. "But you know it's only a question of time before they catch up with you. Even in remote places."

"They do, don't they?" she said. "Ah, well. What time does the Clipper leave in the evening?"

I missed the rest of the conversation because it was time for lunch. Afterwards I told Jenny what I'd heard, and she said I should write down every word in my reporter's notebook. When I did that I realized I'd picked up a lot of clues from that short conversation.

I'd found out the man came from Seattle on the boat called the Victoria Clipper. And the twins were right. People were after the woman, and she had to move from place to place to escape them. It sure looked as if she'd done something wrong.

After that, I always tried to work at Satis Lodge on Wednesday so that I could hear things, and I worked near the house. After I finished, I went to Somecot and wrote down everything in my notebook. On one side of the page I wrote down the conversation. On the other I wrote what I'd found out and what questions I had.

"Do you have to catch the red eye?" the woman said one Wednesday.

"Unfortunately, yes," Mr. Clipper said.

"Poor you! Is there no other way?"

"I've checked. If I don't catch the red eye, there'll be hell to pay."

"I'm afraid I'm a bit of a headache," she said. "I make your life very complicated."

The column with questions was twice as long as the column with facts.

FACTS

– The visitor comes every Wednesday on the Clipper from Seattle.

– The woman either has headaches or causes the man to have headaches.

– She has to move from place to place because people are after her.

– He has to catch a red eye if he doesn't want to get into trouble.

QUESTIONS

– Who is after her? The police or detectives? Good guys or bad guys?

– What has she done to make them come after her?

– What's in the cardboard boxes?

– Who is Mr. Clipper?

– Who or what is the red eye?

– Why does Mr. Clipper have to catch him or it?

– What will happen to Mr. Clipper if he isn't able to catch one?

I tried to find out the answers by asking people some of the questions, without telling them why I was asking.

"Do you know what a red eye is?" I asked Dad.

"Sounds like an eye that's got bloodshot from goggling at television too long. Or do you mean pink eye? That's a very nasty eye infection. I got it once."

"Do you know what a red eye is?" I asked Lisa at the fish counter in the supermarket.

"No," she said. "I know what a gold-eye is, though. Winnipeg gold-eye. Haven't seen much of that for a bit, but I have some nice halibut, fresh in today."

"Maybe the red eye's the name of a person with a bloodshot eye," Jenny said. "Maybe Red Eye's one of the people who's after her."

One Wednesday I managed to hear something when the woman was seeing Mr. Clipper off at the gate.

"Let me take you out to lunch next week," he said. "There's a fine restaurant just down the road."

"It's too much of a risk."

"You must be feeling like a prisoner, darling," he said.

"I'm not as isolated and alone here as I was in the last place. I'm not totally cut off from my fellow human beings."

"That's good," he said, "but be careful!"

They kissed, and then he got into his car and drove off. I noticed that it was a rented car.

When I told all this to Jenny she said that proved he was in love with her, but I didn't agree. Lots of people call each other darling when they aren't in love, and lots of people kiss when they're just friends.

"It all depends whether it's a peck on the cheek or a lingering kiss on the mouth," Jenny said.

"Well, he didn't have time to give her a lingering kiss," I said, "because he was just rushing off to catch the Clipper."

The list of questions seemed to grow longer as we talked about them. And I decided I'd have to work a whole lot harder at being an investigative reporter if I was going to come up with answers to them all.

# 6
# MISTAKES

MRS. T. WAS VERY strict with everyone in the family except Mum, and we were all changing our ways. Timmy was her favorite, but she didn't put up with any nonsense from him, either.

"I won't eat soup with stuff floating in it," he said one day, and I waited to see what she'd do. She just glared while Dad took a slotted spoon, lifted out the floating pieces of broccoli and put them in his own bowl, but she didn't say anything.

"No wonder you're such a shrimp," I said.

The next day she gave us tomato soup with goldfish crackers floating in it.

"Neat," I said.

"Why didn't I get any little fishes?" Timmy complained.

"Because you don't eat soup with stuff floating in it," she said.

"I like fish crackers," he said.

"That's too bad," she said. "I can't remember everybody's likes and dislikes, especially when they change from one day to the next."

"I've changed my mind about soup," Timmy said. "I like stuff floating in it now."

"I'll try to remember that next time," she said.

"Oh, my God, what a mess!" Dad said one day, when he spilled coffee all over his newspaper.

"Thou shalt not take the name of the Lord thy God in vain," Mrs. T. said. "The Lord will not hold him guiltless that taketh his name in vain."

"Sorry, Mrs. T. I'll try to remember that," Dad said.

She made me hang up my clothes instead of throwing them on a chair, she made me sew buttons back on when they came off, and we were always washing our hands because cleanliness was next to godliness.

So when Toby came down to Somecot to tell me Mrs. T. wanted to see me, my knees shook a bit as I ran up to the house.

"You're in *big* trouble, Ellen," he called after me.

I checked off all my chores in my head. I'd made

my bed, sewn a button on my sweater, and I'd tidied up my room pretty well.

When I went into the kitchen, Mrs. T. was rolling out the dough for a rhubarb pie.

"You're in very big trouble with Mrs. Banks," she said. "She just called and she's fit to be tied. You'd better call her back."

"Hello, Mrs. Banks," I said. "Is it about the garden?" I knew I'd been neglecting some of my gardening customers.

"No, it is *not*, Ellen," Mrs. Banks said in an angry voice. "I have issues with you about the muffins."

"What muffins?"

"The muffin recipe in your paper. I tried to make them this morning and the batter ran all over the oven. I just wanted to let you know that I wasted a free-range egg and good butter, not to mention flour, milk *and* a box of expensive blackberries. How *could* you be so careless?" She also told me I got Rover's age wrong in the paper. Then she slammed down the phone.

"Ellen, are you sure you copied out the recipe correctly?" Dad said.

"I read it out to Jenny, and she typed it up on her mother's computer," I said.

Then I remembered that while we were doing it,

Cathy came in and told us about the soap in the fish pond. We talked to her for about half an hour, then we went back and finished the typing. We were both thinking about the fish and wondering who could have done such a stupid thing. We must have mixed up the amounts for the milk and the flour.

Jenny came rushing over when I called her, and we tried to decide what to do.

We decided the best thing was to write the correct recipe on cards and take them around to all the people who had copies of the paper before any more of them tried to make the muffins.

"Anyone who bakes knows that a cup and a half of milk would be too much," Mrs. Fenwick said.

"Well, here's the correct recipe," I said, "and a paper clip so that you can clip it to the paper."

"I've used the same recipe for years out of a cookbook I got for a wedding present forty years ago, and I'm not about to change now. My recipe calls for buttermilk and nutmeg. And it's not necessary to use butter in muffins. Margarine does just as well. But while you're here, Ellen, I must tell you I was very annoyed with what you wrote in your paper about our pets."

"You were?"

"Well, not about Elvis. That was very nice. But when you asked what other animals or birds we had,

I didn't expect you to go and put every single one of their names in your paper. I was just thinking aloud. Goodness, Ellen, you made it look as if we killed them off. We're going to have the humane society after us."

Mr. Weeks said he didn't need the recipe. There was no point going to the trouble of messing up the kitchen and heating up the stove when they had perfectly good muffins at the bakery. Mr. Phillips said he never made them from scratch. He got a box of muffin mix from the supermarket. All you had to do was add an egg and a bit of milk. Mrs. Boyle said she hated blackberry muffins because the seeds get under her dentures.

Miss Jane Green at the library thanked us for bringing the correct recipe, because she fully intended to use it when the blackberries ripened.

"I enjoyed your paper very much in some respects, Ellen," she said, "but I feel bound to tell you that it's full of mistakes. I've counted five spelling mistakes so far. Remember it's '*i* before *e* except after *c*.' And until has only one l. The seasons of the year — spring, summer, fall and winter — don't have capital letters. Unique means one of a kind, so you can say Partridge Cove is very different from other places, but you cannot say it is very unique. If you don't have a dictionary at home, you can use the ones we have in the library."

It was a very discouraging morning. After we talked to Miss Jane Green, we realized how hard it is to put out a paper that doesn't have any mistakes. We felt like giving up right then and there, but we couldn't stop now because we'd have to return the subscription money, and we'd already spent a big chunk of it on our lunch.

When we saw Mr. Higginson crossing the parking lot at the shopping center, we were almost afraid to talk to him. But we thought we'd be in even more trouble if he or Mrs. Higginson used the muffin recipe. He didn't seem angry, though. He said they weren't doing much baking at the moment because they'd just got a new baby, and they had their hands full with him.

"But I'm glad I ran into you," he said, "because you seem to have forgotten some of the grammar rules we took up this past year."

"I know," I said. "Miss Jane Green already pointed them all out to us."

"Oh, she did, did she? Well, we can't have that. Next she'll be complaining to the school board, and I'll be in trouble. Why don't you get your bikes and come over to my house one afternoon? Perhaps I can give you some tips on how to be good journalists."

# 7
# A MEETING

THE NEXT DAY I went to work on one of the narrow gravel paths that winds through the shrubbery at the side of Satis Lodge. Mr. Clipper hadn't arrived yet, so there were no conversations to listen to. As usual I was thinking about the next issue of the paper, and all the work we had to do before it was ready. So I was moving along with my nose to the ground more or less, when I saw a pair of shoes in front of me.

"So this is our new gardener," a voice above me said. It was the voice that had called out the day I went to ask if I could work there. I hadn't heard anyone walking down the path, and I was so surprised that I sat down on the gravel, losing my balance.

"Did I startle you?" the voice said.

"That's okay."

I looked up and saw a tall woman, all in black, with silvery hair mostly hidden under a wide-brimmed hat. I couldn't tell her age because she was wearing dark glasses, but her voice was a young woman's voice.

"And what is your name?" she said.

"Ellen Fremedon."

"Ah, yes. Fremedon. Well, I must say you do a very good job, Ellen Fremedon. Much better than the Green Thumb people."

"Yes," I said. "It's not a good idea to let them spray the weeds. The spray's poisonous, and the poison gets into the ground and seeps into the water in the inlet and kills the fishes. It also kills the insects and butterflies and upsets the whole balance of nature."

"I see," she said. "And how did you learn so much about gardening?" She sat down on one of the large rocks beside the path, pulled a pack of cigarettes out of her pocket and lit a long brown one.

When I saw that, I figured there wasn't much point talking to her about poisons.

"From my mother," I said. "She's very good at gardening. At least she was when she could still get into the garden."

"I've noticed that you have a nice little garden. I often look down at it from my window."

"Little?" I said. "Our garden's over an acre!"

"My!" she said, laughing. "Over an acre! What would you say about a property that was a thousand acres?"

"I'd say you'd need a whole lot of gardeners."

"Not if it wasn't all cultivated," she said. "Most of it was just grassland — as far as the eye could see."

"Were there horses and cows in the fields?" I said, thinking that maybe it was a kind of farm.

"No cows," she said. "But everyone rode horses, and there were flocks of sheep. Plenty of sheep."

"What was it called?" I said.

"What?" she said, as if I'd asked a very difficult question.

"The place that was a thousand acres. Did it have a name?" I wondered if she had trouble with her memory like Gran.

"Pemberley," she said finally. "The name was Pemberley."

Then she looked as if she'd suddenly remembered something important she had to do. She got up quickly and walked off toward the house without saying goodbye. She'd thrown her cigarette down on the ground, so I picked it up and put it in my bucket with the weeds.

Mr. Clipper arrived a bit later, but they stayed in the house and didn't sit on the patio. I was excited, though, and I couldn't wait to tell Jenny that I'd finally met the mysterious stranger.

After that, I had plenty of chances to talk to her because she often came to talk to me when I was working. She always wore dark glasses, even on days when there was no sun.

"Find out as much as you can about her," Jenny said.

"I don't want her to think I'm nosy," I said. "She might decide she doesn't want me working there anymore."

"Well, you are nosy," Jenny said. "Just be your usual self. Ask her if she's lonely, and if she misses her big garden, and stuff like that."

I tried to follow Jenny's instructions, but the problem was the new neighbor asked me so many questions that it was hard for me to ask her any. When I did, she always had to think for a long time before she answered, even if they were really simple questions. Even when I asked what her name was, she thought a long time before she answered.

"You can call me Nerissa," she said.

"Engrossed in thought as always, Ellen Fremedon," she said one day when she'd crept up on me. "A penny for your thoughts."

"I was thinking how nice it must be to live alone."

"Wouldn't you find it lonely after living with a family?"

"A family can really get you down," I said.

"My goodness, Ellen," she said. "So young and such a pessimist. And coming from such a cheerful family."

"Well, it isn't all that cheerful," I said. "The twins drive me crazy, and my grandmother drives my mother crazy, and our housekeeper drives us all crazy…"

"How so?"

"She's very religious, and we're all a bit nervous around her. We're always breaking the Ten Commandments, and she says stuff like 'he that calleth his brother a fool is in danger of hell-fire.' Then Dad says, 'Please, Mrs. T., not so much about hell-fire. It frightens the children.' And she says it's better if the children are frightened now than ending up in it later. They argue about stuff like that at mealtimes. So I think it's better if you live alone, and when you get lonely, you can just ask your friends to come and sleep over."

"Maybe you're right," she said. "But I used to long for solitude, and for everyone to leave me alone. Then when I got the solitude I craved,

I discovered it wasn't as pleasant as I'd expected."

Our conversations were usually short because after we'd been talking for a while, she would go all dreamy, as if she'd floated away from me into another world. Then she'd walk away without saying goodbye. It didn't bother me, though. I thought maybe she was cooking something and had just remembered that a pan was boiling over.

One day when we were talking, I told her I had to leave, and I started packing up my tools. I'd promised to weed the boxes on Mrs. Fenwick's patio so that she could plant pansies. She'd already bought the pansies and they were beginning to dry out. And we were going to plant a sunflower on Elvis's grave.

"You must know everyone in the village and have lots of friends," Nerissa said.

"I do know everyone," I said, "but I don't have many friends."

"And why is that?"

"Most of the kids think I'm a freak, and that our whole family is a freak show," I said. As soon as I said it, I wished I hadn't because I didn't want to go into a lot of details. But she didn't ask any more questions.

"Friends can be a problem," she said. "Look,

Ellen, I have one or two friends who might try to seek me out, and drop in without calling ahead of time. This house is hard to find. If you see anyone asking for me in the village, or looking for two women who have just moved here, would you do me a favor?"

"Give them directions to your house?"

"No, no! That's just what I don't want you to do. I hate to have people dropping in unexpectedly. If you see someone trying to find me, would you come and tell me so that I can have some advance warning?"

"Sure."

"You won't forget, will you?"

"No," I said. "I always follow directions."

"Of course you do," she said. "And you won't tell anyone I asked this, will you, because it might sound as if I'm unfriendly."

I said I wouldn't tell, but I thought it was all right to tell Jenny, because she wouldn't pass it on.

"I think it's obvious what happened," Jenny said. "She was married to a rich man who lived in a mansion with acres of beautiful gardens full of fountains and statues, and sheep in the fields all around. But she fell in love with someone else, and met him secretly with the help of that old woman, who must be her maid. Then the husband found out, and she and the old woman had to run away so that the husband and his spies couldn't find her."

"What about Mr. Clipper?" I said. "I don't think she's in love with him."

"Maybe he's her brother, or someone who's on her side," Jenny said. "And maybe that box he brings is full of letters from her lover."

"It's too big a box just for letters," I said.

"It could have boxes of chocolate and presents in it, too. Or clothes, so the women can disguise themselves and escape if the husband and his spies find out where they are."

"And where does the Red Eye come into it? Do you think he's one of the husband's spies?"

"Probably," Jenny said.

"I wonder what'll happen when Mr. Clipper catches him?"

"I think he'll meet Nerissa, and see how nice she is. Then he'll switch sides, and help her escape from the husband."

Sometimes I think Jenny should be a writer instead of an artist.

# 8
# A VISIT

I T WAS A LONG way to Higg's house, and we were very hot and tired when we got there. He was walking up and down outside his house, carrying a baby that was crying very loudly.

"Hi, there, you two," he said. "If you just hold the baby, I'll go and get some lemonade."

He tried to hand me the baby, but Jenny took it instead because she knows I can't stand babies. She jiggled it up and down, but the baby wouldn't stop crying. I thought it was going to be very hard to talk to Higg if the baby didn't shut up. When he came back with the tray of lemonade and cookies, Higg said the baby was teething. It was drooling, and it had a plastic teething ring dangling from a string around its neck.

"When our twins were teething, Dad used to give them spoons to put in their mouths," I said. "They liked that because the spoons were cold." There was a spoon on the tray so I dipped it in the cold lemonade and gave it to the baby. It stuck it in its mouth and stopped crying.

"Hey, Ellen, that's great," Higg said. "Why didn't I think of that?" The baby sucked on the spoon and held out its other hand as if it wanted to come to me.

"Ellen can't stand babies," Jenny said, "and they always want to go to her."

"I think they just want to grab my glasses," I said, thinking Higg might be offended, because most people expect everyone to be crazy about their babies. But Higg didn't seem to mind. I guess he was pretty fed up with the baby, because it had been crying all afternoon. He's a poet and he was trying to finish some new poems for his next book.

"It's just the same with me and cats," he said. "I can't stand them, and they always make a bee-line for me."

"What's the baby's name?" I said.

"His full name is Kennedy Worthington Russell," he said. "But we call him Thumper."

"He's very big for a new baby," I said, "and it's funny that he's teething so soon."

"Well, he's new to us, but he's not a newborn," Higg said. "We just got him."

"Are you fostering him?"

"No, we adopted him. He's ours for ever and ever, aren't you, old boy?"

Thumper just drooled, but finally he fell asleep, and Higg said it looked like we might get a bit of peace at last. There was a buggy under a tree, and Higg put Thumper into it.

"Aren't you supposed to put a net over the buggy?" I said. "There's a lot of yellow jackets around this year."

"Good thinking, Ellen." He brought a mosquito net out of the house and put it over the buggy. He said his wife was taking a summer course in computers, and he was supposed to be keeping the home fires burning, but he couldn't get anything done because Thumper was taking up so much of his time.

It was nice sitting on the grass under a big oak tree and drinking lemonade. The grass went all the way down to the inlet, and there was a breeze coming off the water. We told Higg about all the trouble we'd had since we delivered the first issue of our paper — the complaints about spelling, and the obituary notices, and the muffin recipe with the wrong ingredients, and how mad Mrs. Banks was.

"Well, there's a long history of journalists getting into trouble," he said. "It goes with the job." Then he told us how some of the first journalists had ended up in prison for writing things that annoyed the king or queen or whoever was running England at the time.

"Daniel Defoe was a journalist before he wrote *Robinson Crusoe*," Higg said. "When he was quite a young man he wrote an article saying that people should be allowed to go to any church they wanted — Catholic, Protestant, Methodist, Presbyterian, you name it. That was a pretty brave thing to write at the time, because people didn't have freedom of religion. He was fined and put in the pillory."

"What's a pillory?" Jenny said.

"It's a kind of wooden frame with holes for the head and hands so that prisoners can be held there while people insult them or throw things at them. Sometimes prisoners had their ears cut off when they were pilloried."

"Did Daniel Defoe have his ears cut off?" I said.

"No," Higg said. "As a matter of fact, putting him in the pillory backfired. The people liked his ideas so much that they cheered him and brought flowers instead. He became a hero. But not all journalists were so lucky."

"Did they all write things that bugged the kings and queens?"

"Not by any means," Higg said. "They wrote essays on all kinds of different subjects. And stories. Whole books were published bit by bit in some papers, so that people who couldn't afford to buy books could read them there. There was a lot of excitement waiting for the next episode."

"If we make up stories and put them in the paper, we won't get into trouble by offending people," I said.

"But you will get into trouble if you don't improve the spelling and grammar," Higg said. "You'll have Miss Jane Green on your case all the time."

"It's hard to catch all the mistakes when you only have two weeks to fill a whole newspaper," I said.

"That's another problem that all journalists have," Higg said. "That's why they have copy-editors."

"What's a copy-editor?"

"It's someone whose job it is to go over what somebody else has written and try to catch all the mistakes in spelling, grammar, punctuation, capitalization, etc.," Higg said.

"Will you be our copy-editor?" Jenny said.

"We'll give you a free subscription," I said.

"Thanks for the offer," said Higg, "but I've got my hands full here. Thumper will be waking up any minute and wanting food, and drink, and a diaper change, and a bath, and goodness knows what else."

"Why don't we take care of Thumper while you copy-edit the paper?" Jenny said.

If we'd been sitting at a table instead of on the grass, I'd have given her a good kick. I didn't want to spend my summer afternoons looking after some baby that was teething, and changing its diapers.

"I'll do the next best thing," Higg said. "I'll give you each a grammar handbook. You have fax machines at home, don't you? Well, you fax your paper to me before it goes to press…"

"It doesn't go to press," I said. "We just photocopy it at the library."

"Well, you fax me your rough draft. I'll mark all the spelling and grammar mistakes. But you have to use your grammar books and your dictionaries to correct the mistakes."

"How will we know what the mistakes are?" I said.

Instead of answering, he went into the house. When he came back, he gave us each a copy of a grammar handbook. Inside the back page it said Revision Symbols. Higg said there were symbols for all the mistakes we were likely to make — sp for spelling, frag for a sentence that didn't have a verb, and a whole lot more. He would pick out our mistakes and put the symbol in the margin. Then we could look up the mistake in the grammar book and correct it.

It all sounded pretty complicated, but we thanked him anyway.

Just then a truck drove up, and Mrs. Higginson got out. Higg introduced us, and told her why we had come over.

"I've just offered to proofread their paper," he said.

"I always proofread the stuff he writes," she said.

We were surprised that a teacher would make so many mistakes that he needed a proofreader. He explained that it's very hard to catch your own mistakes, and much easier for someone else to spot them.

"How was Thumper?" she said.

"Raised Cain most of the afternoon." Higg said, "Then the girls arrived, and Ellen managed to get him settled down."

"I'm glad to see you remembered the mosquito

net," she said. "The poor thing got two mosquito bites the last time you put him down for a nap outside."

"Oh, I wasn't likely to make that mistake again," Higg said.

Then Mrs. Higg said she had to go into the village to pick up something for their supper. She said that we could put our bikes in the back of the truck, and she'd take us as far as the village. We were pretty happy to get a ride, because it was getting late.

"Hey, why don't we have a Births column in the paper, and put Thumper in it?" Jenny said, as we were pushing our bikes up the hill from the village.

"Great idea!"

# 9
# NEXT ISSUE

THE NEXT DAY WE had an editorial meeting in Somecot. First we talked about the mistakes in the last issue and how we could apologize to the people we'd offended so that they wouldn't cancel their subscriptions. I said I'd bake a batch of muffins and take them to Mrs. Banks to make up for all the stuff she'd wasted.

Then we talked about what should go in the next issue. We'd had another talk with Cathy about the ongoing investigation of the vandalism. She said there was nothing new, and we couldn't write about likely suspects when we had no evidence. So we decided that unless we got a good news story for the front page, the next issue of the paper would be only two pages long instead of four. We hoped people wouldn't complain about not getting their money's worth.

None of the neighbors or their pets had died so there would be no Obituaries, but Jenny said there were two items for the Births column. Besides Thumper, the cat belonging to Pat at the bookstore had just had kittens. Jenny said she'd find out their names, and if Pat had found homes for them. I thought we should call the column Special Occasions so it could include births, deaths, birthday parties, accidents, and any other important events that happened to neighbors or their pets. Mr. Wilkins had been in bed with a bad attack of sciatica, but we decided not to put that in because we'd found that people can be very touchy when you write about them in the paper.

Jenny said we should have an Arts section, with some of the book reports we did in school, if we could find them. I got an A for a book report on *The Diary of Anne Frank*, and Jenny got a B+ for a report on a book about Emily Carr. I said it would be a good idea to have an interview with a writer. Higg was the only one we knew, and we thought he would agree to be interviewed, if Jenny looked after Thumper. I said I would call him up and ask when we could do it.

After the meeting, I went back to the house and

made a batch of muffins and took them around to Mrs. Banks.

"Oh, Ellen," she said, "that's very kind of you. Perhaps I shouldn't have been so angry about your recipe. But I was raised on the prairies during the depression, and I just can't stand to see food wasted."

"That's okay," I said. "My gran's the same way."

"I don't throw anything away," Mrs. Banks said. She pointed to five loaves of banana bread lined up on the kitchen table.

"Bananas go off very quickly in this hot weather, and these bananas peaked two days ago. Mr. Banks refuses to eat them when they're overripe so I freeze the speckled ones and make them into banana bread. I make a lot of loaves at the same time because they freeze very well. Would you like a slice?"

She gave me a slice of banana bread and a glass of milk. It was very good and it gave me an idea. I asked Mrs. Banks if she would give me the recipe for our paper. I promised I'd be very careful and make no mistakes with it. So we had a recipe for the next issue.

"By the way, Ellen," she said, "I'm glad you came round. I wanted to tell you that I had a very nice note from Doris Fenwick. She didn't even know that we'd lost Rover, and I didn't know that Elvis had died. She's coming over for coffee very soon, so your paper has done a good thing in bringing us together."

I was about to tell her about journalists making mistakes when Mr. Banks came in. He was out of breath and his face was a lot redder than usual.

"You know that little maple tree they planted by the bench at the bus stop?" he said.

"I do," said Mrs. Banks. "It's going to be a long time before it provides any shade for people waiting for the bus."

"It's never going to provide any shade," he said, "because someone's destroyed it."

"Why would anyone want to do that?"

"I don't know," Mr. Banks said. "It was a senseless act of vandalism. Some jerk cut it off halfway down and left a stump sticking up. Mrs. Boyd was passing by, and she had the nerve to blame our Cathy. She said if the police were doing their duty instead of taking coffee breaks all the time, there wouldn't be so much vandalism."

"And if the parents and the school were doing their duty, there wouldn't be so many vandals," Mrs. Banks said. "There was none of this when I was growing up. When we weren't in school, we were all so busy with our chores we had no time to hang around and get into mischief."

I thought maybe I should take the hint and stop hanging around, so I said I'd better be going. Mrs. Banks wrote out her banana loaf recipe and gave me a loaf to take home.

### MRS. BANKS' BANANA BREAD

*2 eggs*
*1 cup sugar*
*3 over-ripe bananas*
*1/4 cup oil*
*3 teaspoons baking soda*
*a pinch of salt*
*1 1/2 cups white flour*
*1/2 cup sour milk or buttermilk*

*Beat the eggs, and then mix the eggs and sugar together. Mash the over-ripe bananas and add them to the mixture. Mix in the oil.*

*Add the baking soda and the salt to the flour. Stir a little flour into the mixture and then a little milk and keep on adding them until they are all used up.*

*Line a loaf pan with a piece of buttered parchment paper. Pour the mixture into the pan. Bake at 275 degrees for 2 1/2 hours.*

*Mrs. Banks says 2 1/2 hours is a long time*

*to keep the oven on so make several loaves at the same time.*

As I walked home, I had another idea. Editorials in the paper are often about bad things that happen. This latest vandalism would make a good subject for an editorial in our next issue. So I went straight down to Somecot and wrote it out:

### *PARTRIDGE COVE VANDAL STRIKES AGAIN*

*There has been some more vandalism in Partridge Cove. First, the fish in the ornamental pond were poisoned by detergent and now the maple tree by the bus stop has been destroyed.*

*It was a good little tree that was planted two years ago and it was doing very well. We thought it might not last through the first winter when it snowed and was cold, but it did. It lasted through the dry summer weather, even though nobody bothered to water it or put any fertilizer on it. Dogs used it for a toilet, and that didn't kill it. So it grew quite a bit in two years. Then someone went and cut it off leaving just a bare stump. This was a senseless act.*

*We can all help to stop vandals. If you see anybody acting suspicious, take down the license number of their car or motorbike. Try to remember what the people look like, and then call Cathy Banks and tell her what you have seen. It is too late to save the fish and the maple tree but you may stop something else from being vandalized.*

I was pretty pleased with the editorial. Then I wondered if I should have mentioned that dogs peed on the tree. I thought it might upset Mrs. Banks, because Rover was always doing that, so I scratched it out.

All in all, the visit to the Banks' house was really useful because I got a recipe and an editorial out of it. I realized that if you were a journalist, there was a lot to be said for just hanging around and talking to people.

# 10
# PAPARAZZI

I T WAS EASIER THAN I thought to sell a newspaper subscription to Nerissa, because the subject just came up naturally when she was talking to me one day.

"Tell me, Ellen," she said. "What do you do when you aren't working in people's gardens? Do you go swimming or play tennis?"

"Sometimes," I said, "but I don't like sports much because I can't see the ball very well and I can't see without my glasses in the water. And I don't have a lot of time because Mum's ill and I have to help out with the laundry and cooking and gardening."

"So it's all work and no play! You don't have any hobbies?"

"Well, this summer I'm working on a newspaper that comes out every two weeks. I'm the editor-in-chief, and Jenny's the business manager and art director."

"Good heavens!" she said. "Don't tell me I've allowed a journalist into my garden!"

She sounded really shocked, as if a journalist was something bad. So I explained to her about the lies and rumors about our family that had appeared in the papers last year, and how we had started a paper that would tell the truth.

"Well, that's a relief," she said. "I thought for a moment you were a paparazzo."

"A what?"

"It's an Italian word for journalists who buzz around famous people like mosquitoes and make their lives miserable. They follow them everywhere, spying on them, getting details of their personal lives, and taking photographs of them in private moments."

"Why would they do that?"

"Well, the big newspapers pay millions of dollars for photographs and stories about the secret lives of rich and famous people, so the paparazzi try all kinds of tricks to get them."

"What kinds of tricks?"

"Oh, they've been known to dress up as Santa

Claus and wait outside the apartment buildings of famous people to take photographs of them. They get themselves hired as waiters in restaurants so they can listen to conversations, and they've even gone as far as getting hired as maids and workers in their homes."

"They have?"

"They even get special miniature cameras that can be easily hidden, or ones with telescopic lenses that can take photographs from a great distance away."

"Well, there aren't any famous people in Partridge Cove," I said, "and I don't have a camera. So I can't be a para…"

"Paparazzo. Even if there were famous people here, you wouldn't want to spy on them, to get stories and pictures that would embarrass them, would you?"

"I don't think so," I said. "But it would be nice to make lots of money."

"And what would you do with all that money?"

"I'd go to the Creamery for lunch all the time. And I'd buy a greenhouse for my mother, so that she could keep on gardening in her wheelchair."

After that, I asked Nerissa if she'd like to buy our newspaper.

"I'd like that very much," she said.

"You can buy separate copies, or you can buy a three-month subscription and I could bring you all the back issues."

"I think I'd like a three-month subscription," she said. "Make that two subscriptions. I think my friend would be interested in your newspaper, too."

"The first issue isn't very good," I said. "We made a lot of mistakes because we didn't have a proofreader then."

"And you have one now?"

"Higg, our teacher from last year, proofreads the paper and marks the mistakes. Then we look them up in a grammar book and correct them. He writes poetry and I'm going to interview him for the Arts section."

"Well, I'm very much looking forward to reading your paper," she said.

So, after I'd finished the weeding, I went home and got the papers we'd published so far, and she paid me for them.

Jenny was really happy about the subscriptions. Then I told her about the paparazzi and their dirty tricks. I said I felt terrible because that's exactly what I was doing, and I thought I should stop working in her garden.

"Well, you can't just tell her you won't work

there anymore," Jenny said. "She'd find that highly suspicious. Besides, Ellen, you don't seem to find out very much anyway. It seems to me you always talk about your life. She's the one who asks all the nosy questions and wants to find out all about you."

That was true. Nerissa was very curious about my family. She asked about Mum's illness, and Dad's work, and the twins, and about what happened last summer, and about Jenny and Higg and Mrs. T. She didn't seem at all embarrassed about being nosy.

"Tell me more about your housekeeper," she said one day.

"Well, she's very religious, and she talks about the Lord a lot. She says he knows about everything that happens in the world. He sees the little sparrow fall and knows the number of hairs on everybody's head. That scares Timmy and makes him cry, and then Dad has to tell her to stop. She argues with Dad a lot."

"Doesn't that make him angry?"

"Not really," I said. "He's a philosopher so he likes arguing."

"What do they argue about?"

"Well, Mrs. T. says if you don't believe in God and read the Bible and follow the Ten Commandments, you won't know how to tell right from wrong."

"What does he say to that?" Nerissa said.

"He says lots of people do good not because they're afraid God will get mad at them if they don't or reward them if they do but because they have moral standards and want to do the right thing. Something like that. He has a lot of books about telling right from wrong. He tries to lend them to her."

"And does she read them?"

"No. She says she isn't one of those people lucky enough to have time on their hands for reading. The only book she needs is the Holy Bible, and there's enough in it to get her through this world and land her in the next. She only hopes our books will do the same for us."

"Does your mother join in these arguments?" Nerissa said.

"Not much. She doesn't have the energy for arguing. She says she believes in tolerance, good temper and sympathy, and that's enough for her."

"And your grandmother? Does she believe in God?"

"Oh, yes. She says her prayers, and she says grace at mealtimes, but she doesn't go to church. She says you can worship God in a garden better than anywhere else. She has this poem she always recites:

> The kiss of the sun for pardon,
> The song of the birds for mirth,
> One is nearer God's Heart in a garden,
> Than anywhere else on earth."

"But I thought you said your grandmother didn't have a garden. Didn't you tell me she lives in an apartment in the city?" Nerissa said.

"Yes. But Gran isn't logical. She says philosophy's all very well, but it's no substitute for plain common sense."

"And what does your father say about that?" Nerissa said.

"He says Gran has many fine qualities, but logical thinking isn't among them. We're not supposed to point that out, though, because she's an older person and our grandmother. Mum's the only person who's allowed to be rude to her."

"In spite of believing in tolerance, good temper and sympathy?"

"Well, Gran drives her crazy, the way my brother drives me crazy," I said.

"Ah, and what's Timmy been getting up to lately?"

"We hired him to be the delivery boy for our newspaper, and Jenny paid him a nickel for every paper he delivered. But instead of taking them around to the mailboxes, he just stuck them in the library for people to pick up, and a lot of people who hadn't paid for them took them, and we had to spend so much time running off extra copies that we got behind with the next issue. And he spent the money before we could get it back from him."

"This newspaper business causes you so many headaches, I'm surprised you still have time to do gardening jobs," she said.

I just looked at her when she said that. I was thinking that I really didn't have much time for gardening jobs. They were just part of my investigative reporting. I felt guilty all over again.

"I'm very glad you do, though," she said. "I don't know where I should be without you. What I mean to say is, the garden would get completely out of hand."

"I think I should start digging the moss out of the stone wall along the side of the shrubbery," I said.

"What a good idea," she said. "I was just thinking how untidy that wall looks. I'd appreciate it if you could come in more often."

I was glad to do that. There was the investigative

reporting, and the money she paid me, but the main reason was that I really liked talking to her. Sometimes when we were talking I didn't get much weeding done, and the pail of weeds was only about a third full. But she said that didn't matter, and she paid me the full amount for the time I'd been there.

I liked the way she was interested in my life and listened when I complained about my family. I was sure by now that she couldn't have done anything wrong because she was so nice. And I didn't agree with Jenny that Mr. Clipper was someone who was helping her or her lover.

He wasn't nice at all, and I didn't think the boxes were full of presents. More likely he was making her work for him. She had very pretty hands so maybe she did beautiful needlework, and he brought things for her to sew. That would explain why she always walked away in the middle of our conversations. Maybe she remembered the piles of clothes she had to finish before he came. And maybe she lived in fear that something terrible would happen if she didn't get them done on time.

# 11
# INTERVIEWING HIGG

IT WAS A CLEAR, hot afternoon when Jenny and I
set off on our bikes to Higg's place. Jenny was going
to babysit Thumper while I did the interview.

I had Mum's cassette player in my basket,
and the library copy of Higg's book of poetry. He
said when you interview somebody you don't just
ask the first questions that pop into your head. You
have to plan it carefully, and if the person has written a book, you should read it. I also had a notebook, a pen and a list of questions. Jenny had a
mobile she'd made for Thumper in her basket.

Thumper was in his crib when we got there, and
Jenny fixed the mobile to the side of it. The mobile
had a sun, a crescent moon, and some planets and
stars. It went round and round in the breeze from

the open window. Thumper watched it for a while, and then his eyelids drooped, and he fell sound asleep. So Jenny sat in on the interview. We went down to the basement where Higg's desk was set up in a corner near the washing machine.

"I thought you'd need a special room with a nice view for writing poetry," I said.

"I prefer a blank wall over my desk," Higg said. "If there was a view I'd be distracted by it, and I wouldn't be able to concentrate as well."

"Is it hard to write poetry?"

"It's hard to write good poetry," Higg said, "and even harder to write very good poetry. What did you think of the poems in my book?"

"I was surprised they didn't rhyme," I said. "I thought poems were supposed to rhyme."

"Many people think rhyme is the be-all and end-all of poetry," Higg said, "but it's not. It's a bit like that blue top Jenny's wearing …"

I felt bad because I was wearing an ugly T-shirt with I ♥ NEW YORK on the front. It was supposed to be white, but I'd accidentally put it in a colored wash and it had come out gray.

"Rhyme is like that piece of trim round the neck of Jenny's top or that flower thing on the front," Higg said. "What do you call them?"

"The white strip is piping, and this flower is appliqué," Jenny said.

"Well, they aren't actually necessary. They're an extra touch, but they add something and they pick up the color in the rest of the top."

"I thought the flower was a bit too fussy," Jenny said. "I've been thinking of taking it off."

"I sometimes think rhyme is a bit too fussy, and that's why I don't use it," Higg said.

"Do poets always write about things like spring and flowers and birds?" I said.

"Not always. They can write about anything they want," Higg said.

"How do you get ideas for poems?" I said.

"I get inspiration everywhere. From the garden, from teaching my classes, from changing Thumper's diapers…"

"You couldn't write a poem about changing diapers, could you?"

"You could indeed. The unlikeliest subjects often produce the best poems. I also get inspired by reading other writers. In fact, one of your editorials gave me the idea for a poem."

"Which one?"

"The one about the maple tree that was cut down by vandals," Higg said.

"It wasn't a very pretty tree," I said. "Why would it make a good poem?"

"You wrote about someone planting the seed, watering it, tending it and then replanting it by the bus-stop. And how it survived snow storms, and heavy rain, and drought…"

"Dogs were always peeing on it, too," I said, "but I didn't put that in."

"Anyway, you made a little story about the life of the tree, and that story made me think how certain people — gardeners or poets — work to create a thing of beauty. They run into difficulties but they slog away and their work succeeds against all odds. And what they create often appears very fragile and insignificant, but it's stronger than it looks…"

"But the maple tree wasn't strong when the vandal came along with a knife," I said.

"That's true," Higg said. "Sometimes a person comes along who can't stand the sight of a beautiful object. Perhaps it's somebody who doesn't have the skill or patience to make a thing of beauty, and so that somebody destroys it. Destroying is a lot easier than creating."

"Well, it would be a very sad poem if it said that beautiful things are always getting destroyed."

"But it would be hopeful if it urged us not to be

discouraged, but to go on planting trees and creating beautiful objects."

Just then we heard a racket upstairs. Thumper had woken up and started screaming.

"Uh-oh," Higg said. "I didn't answer half your questions. Why don't you leave them with me and I'll fax the answers to you?"

"Wow, look how late it is," Jenny said, looking at her watch. "Ellen has to be home to help with supper."

Higg stood at the door and waved as we left. He was holding Thumper. Boy, could that kid scream.

"Do you think the Higgs wish they hadn't adopted Thumper?" I said.

"Of course not," Jenny said. "He's cute."

It was even hotter than it was when we set out, so we got off our bikes and sat in the shade by the side of the road for a while.

"What sort of jerk would want to cut down a little tree or poison a lot of fish?" Jenny said.

"A person with a grudge against the people of Partridge Cove," I said. "Maybe someone from the city who got a ticket for speeding or littering. I bet Cathy has a list of suspects, but she won't tell us who they are."

Just then we heard a huge roar and saw a motor-bike speeding down the road in a cloud of dust. The man on the bike was all in black leather with a helmet and goggles. He sped past us, and then slowed down, stopped, turned around and came back to us. I was a bit scared. Then he pushed off his helmet and goggles, and we saw that he was an older man with gray hair.

"You girls okay?" he said.

"We're just having a rest," Jenny said.

"That's fine then," he said. "I thought maybe you had trouble with your bikes and needed some help."

He put the helmet and goggles back on and rode off down the road.

"What a nice biker," I said.

# 1 2
# A SHOCK

THE NEXT SUNDAY MORNING was very quiet.
Gran didn't come up to lunch, the twins went with
Cathy Banks to a farm, and Jenny went with her
mother to an opening at the art gallery in the city.
Anne invited me to go with them but Mum wanted
me to stay home and make lunch. Mrs. T. doesn't
come in on Sunday because Sunday is the Sabbath
of the Lord thy God and on it you aren't supposed to
do any work. It's one of the Ten Commandments.

I was working, though, on the next issue of the
paper. That's why I didn't mind staying home.

I'd interviewed a lot of the neighbors about the
vandalism in Partridge Cove, and I spent the morning in Somecot trying to write up what people had
said and thinking of a good headline.

"Teenagers today have too much time on their hands," Mrs. Banks said. "When I was growing up, kids had so many chores, they didn't have time for all this mischief."

"I did a lot of chores," Mr. Banks said, "but I still found time for hell-raising. Boy, did I ever! Wild Bill, they used to call me. You wouldn't believe the things we did on Hallowe'en — soaping windows, tipping over outhouses, tying firecrackers to dogs' tails. One time we had this young schoolteacher…"

"We don't need to hear about that," Mrs. Banks said. She'd just made some butter tarts, and she gave me one and asked me if I'd like the recipe for my paper. I put the recipe in my pocket and went to interview Mrs. Fenwick.

"Kids these days get too much too soon," Mrs. Fenwick said, when I asked her opinion.

"Too much of what?"

"Everything," she said. "You name it."

Mr. Weeks said that in his day every principal had a paddle and every father had a switch and they weren't afraid to use them. If they used them nowadays they'd end up in court. They'd call it child abuse or something. So kids were growing up hog wild, and all this vandalism was the result.

Mr. Phillips said he blamed the government for not cracking down on crime. They let foreigners into the country who don't know how to behave in a civilized place. Miss Jane Green said she thought the schools could do more to teach young people to respect other people's property.

I wondered why they all blamed kids when most of the crimes you read about in the paper are done by grown-ups. I thought I'd ask Mum and Dad about that at lunch. We were just having cold cuts and fruit, so when the bell rang I went up and sliced some tomatoes, onions and radishes and set them on a platter. It's so nice when there's just the three of us at the table, and we can talk without being interrupted.

"Ellen," Dad said, after we'd filled our plates. "There's something we have to tell you."

It's always scary when a conversation starts off like that. I had an awful feeling he was going to say we had to sell the house and move away from Partridge Cove.

"Is it a bad thing?" I said.

"No, not a bad thing. And perhaps it isn't very important. It's just something you should know."

Then they looked at each other, as if to see which one of them should tell me this thing that wasn't very important but I should know. Neither of them seemed to want to go first.

"Well, what is it?" I said.

"You know, Ellen," Mum said, "children come to us in many different ways."

I hoped they weren't going to go on about sex. Jenny and I talk about sex quite a lot, but I hate it when parents do. It's so embarrassing, you don't know where to look.

"I know all about that," I said. "We took it in health at school."

"Sometimes they come when parents are ready for them," Mum went on, as if I hadn't said anything, "and sometimes they come unexpectedly, when parents are not ready for them or able to look after them. All you children were very much wanted. We were very eager to have children."

"Even the twins?"

"Even the twins," Mum said. "But the three of you came to us in different ways."

"We did?"

"Yes. We'd been married for some time, Dad and I, and we badly wanted to start a family."

"Why?"

"Well, it was lonely with just the two of us," Mum said after a while. I thought that sounded pretty suspicious.

"Was it because you needed help with the gardening and cooking?" I said.

"Of course not, Ellen," Mum said. "Babies are a

lot of work. It's a long time before they can be much help in the house and garden, and even then... Anyway, we were very eager to have a baby, and none came along, so we decided to adopt one. And we were lucky enough to find you, Ellen."

"*Find* me? What was I doing when you found me?"

"You were in hospital like most babies when we first saw you," Dad said. "You were just a day old."

"And we thought you were the loveliest little thing in the world," Mum said.

"You said all babies look like little old men," I said.

"As you know, people always think their own babies are beautiful," Mum said.

"But I wasn't your own baby. I don't get this. Where was the person who borned me? Was she dead?"

"Gave birth to you. No, Ellen," Dad said. "She was not in a position to provide a home for a baby, and so she decided to let her baby go to people who were eager to have a baby, and who could provide a home for it."

"For her," Mum said.

"So you're not my real parents," I said.

"Ellen," Dad said, "I can assure you we are very

much your real parents. We wanted you, we found you, we've cared for you from the very beginning…"

"We love you very much," Mum said. "It's just that we are not your birth or biological parents."

"What about the twins?" I said. "Are you their real parents?"

"We are their real parents, just as we are your real parents," Dad said. "We are also their birth parents."

"Why didn't you adopt *them*?" I said.

"They arrived in our lives unexpectedly," Mum said.

"Did you not want any more kids after me?"

"We hadn't expected to have any more, but we were happy to have them. Surprised but happy," Mum said.

"Did you have a lot of babies to choose from when you picked me?" I asked.

"It wasn't a question of picking you out, Ellen," Mum said. "We asked if it was possible to adopt a baby. We waited quite a long time, and then we were very pleased to be told that you could be our daughter."

"Who told you about me?"

"Well, the adoption agency," Dad said.

"Suppose the family doesn't like the kid they've

adopted. Can they take it back to the hospital and exchange it?"

"That just doesn't happen, Ellen," Mum said, "any more than parents take the children they've given birth to back to the hospital. Having a child is a life-long commitment."

"Who else knows I'm adopted?"

"Well, Gran does, of course," Dad said.

"Although I think by this time Gran has quite forgotten how you came to us," Mum said.

"So everyone in the family knew except me. Why didn't you tell me? I had a right to know."

"That may be true," Dad said. "But when you were old enough to understand, the twins suddenly arrived, and we were busy looking after them. Then Mum became ill, and somehow…it didn't seem important. Nothing has changed. You're our daughter, no matter how you arrived."

After lunch, I went to my room and lay on my bed. It made me mad to think that everyone knew something about me that I hadn't known. Dad always made a big deal about telling the truth, but he hadn't been so truthful with me. Not telling me I was adopted was the same as telling me a lie.

I thought about Dad saying nothing had changed. That was another big lie. Everything had changed. For one thing, I'd never believe anything they told me ever again.

Then I started wondering what it would have been like if someone else had adopted me. I could have been adopted by a rich family, and had great clothes and vacations in Hawaii, and lived in a big house and had a horse.

Or I might have been adopted by a poor family and not had enough to eat. I thought the person I would really like to have been adopted by was Higg. Too bad I hadn't been at the hospital when he went to get Thumper.

Next I began to wonder if Mum and Dad ever wished they'd picked out a different baby, one that turned out to be pretty like Jenny, and talented at drawing and painting, instead of an ugly kid with bad eyesight who was lousy at sports. I wondered if they were telling the truth about why my real mother gave me away. Maybe she took one look at me and decided she didn't like me.

There were so many thoughts going around my head that when Dad tapped on my door and said Jenny was on the phone, I told him to tell her I wasn't feeling well. I didn't even want to go upstairs for supper, but Dad said there was cake and ice cream for dessert, so I thought I might as well.

The twins were jabbering on about their outing

with Cathy. They'd seen some llamas, and some emus, and they'd helped to milk a goat. It all sounded pretty boring to me.

"The llamas protect the sheep from cougars and dogs," Toby said.

"They spit at things when they don't like the look of them," Timmy said.

"Well, they must have spit all over you then," I said.

"Ellen's mad because she didn't get to see the farm."

"Why don't you just shut up about the stupid farm," I said.

"Timmy, please," said Mum. "Stop pestering Ellen. She isn't feeling very well today."

"That's probably because she's been stuffing her face with ice cream all day."

"All right, Timmy, that's enough," Dad said. "Any more of that and you'll have to leave the table."

And I began to see that something had changed, after all. For once Mum and Dad were sticking up for me because I knew I was adopted, instead of always being on the twins' side because I was older, and I was supposed to know better.

# 1 3
# CONFIDENCES

THE NEXT DAY I woke up to the usual morning noises and smells. I heard the coffee grinder and smelled Dad's coffee and burning toast. But something didn't feel right. I rummaged around in my mind to find what it was. The editorial I still hadn't written for the next issue of the paper?

Then I remembered about being adopted. I felt weird all over again when I thought I wasn't the same person that I'd been when I woke up the day before.

Just as I was eating my cereal Jenny called to see if I was okay.

"You should have come to the opening with us," she said. "They had little shrimps on toothpicks that you dipped in a sauce. And there was a lady playing a harp."

I said I wished I'd gone with them.

"Did you finish your editorial?" she said.

"No."

She said she'd come over and show me her drawings for the next issue, and I said I'd meet her in Somecot.

"Did you have an upset stomach?" Jenny said when she came in. "You look a bit peaky."

I'd decided to tell Jenny about being adopted, but I wanted to think about it some more first. I didn't feel like talking about it right away.

"Maybe you had sunstroke," Jenny said. "Oh, that reminds me. I was at the Clothes Loft and I saw the cutest baby sunhat. It was on sale because most people have bought their sunhats by now. I was wondering if we could take some money out of the bank account and buy it for Thumper. It was yellow and sort of like an upside-down buttercup with a cute little green stem on the top."

I'd been thinking about Thumper a lot since yesterday, and when Jenny mentioned him like that out of the blue, it threw me.

"Why are you looking at me all funny?" Jenny said. "It was just an idea. Though I guess we shouldn't be spending any more money."

"Jenny," I said, "you know Thumper was adopted?"

"Sure," Jenny said. "That's why he's teething even though he's a new baby. He was six months old when they got him."

"I was adopted," I said. Her mouth dropped open.

"You never told me that before."

"I didn't find out till yesterday."

"Are you sure it's true? Everybody says you're just like your dad."

"I don't look like him," I said.

"But you talk just like him. Nobody *looks* just like their dad."

"Well, it's true," I said. "Mum and Dad told me yesterday. They said they'd been married a long time, and they wanted kids and they weren't able to have any, so they went to the adoption agency and got me."

"What about the twins?" she said. "Were they adopted?"

"No. They got born normally. After they adopted me, they found out they were able to have kids, after all."

"Wow!"

"So I'm wondering now if Mum and Dad are sorry they went to the trouble of adopting me. After the twins were born, maybe they thought they should have waited a bit longer."

Tears started leaking out my eyes.

"Oh, Ellen!"

"Maybe they'd rather have a kid that's their own flesh and blood and born the normal way. They're always saying how messy I am, and clumsy. And my glasses are a big expense. And on top of everything else I may have to get braces."

"On the other hand, you help out a lot around the house," Jenny said.

"That's another thing," I said. "I do more than anyone else, and I never get any thanks. It's just Ellen take the clothes out of the dryer and fold them up and Ellen peel the potatoes. It was just my rotten luck I got chosen by Mum and Dad."

"I've always thought you were lucky, because at least you have a regular family. My mom and dad split up, and my dad married again, and I got a stepmother who doesn't like having me around, and a baby stepbrother I never get to see. I see Thumper more often than I see my real brother."

"Brothers aren't all that great," I said. "You've got a nice family with Anne and Cathy."

"It wasn't such a good thing when Cathy moved in with us," Jenny said.

"It wasn't? I thought you liked having Cathy there."

"I did at first. And Cathy's okay but it causes a

lot of problems for me. A lot of the kids at school say it's sick that Mom lives with another woman. And Mrs. T. can't stand having me around."

"Dad says that's narrow-minded," I said. "He says narrow-minded people don't like anyone that's different from them, and that causes a lot of the trouble in the world."

"Well, it causes a lot of trouble in my life, and I don't like it," Jenny said. "Besides, I get upset when Mom and Cathy fight."

"I didn't know that. They always seem nice when I come over."

"Well, families always seem nice when other people come over," Jenny said. "Even Mom and Dad used to stop fighting when they had company."

"What do Anne and Cathy fight about?"

"Just now it's about a dog. Cathy wants a big one that would scare off robbers. She says there's a lot of breaking and entering going on in the valley. And Mom says she'd be the one that would have to clean up after a dog. She's a cat person, anyway."

We both got very quiet, thinking about our problems.

"Do you remember that time when we thought of an advice column called Ask Aunt Partridge, for people with problems?" Jenny said. "And we were going to write letters ourselves to get the thing started?"

"Yes," I said, "but we couldn't think of any problems to write about."

"Well, we have problems now," Jenny said. "Maybe we should each write to Aunt Partridge, and then the other one could reply," Jenny said. "Nobody would know it was us because we'd just sign ourselves Miserable or Worried."

"Hey, that's a great idea." So we each got a piece of paper and wrote a letter.

Jenny wrote:

*Dear Aunt Partridge,*
*My mom lives with another woman and the kids at school think that's sick, and they take it out on me. Also my mom and her partner keep arguing about getting a dog. C. says a big dog would protect us from B & E's. Mom says she couldn't stand the mess a big dog would make. These problems are getting me down, and some days I feel like running away from home.*

*Unhappy, Partridge Cove*

I wrote:

*Dear Aunt Partridge,*
*I've just learned that my parents adopted me*
*because they thought they weren't able to*
*have kids of their own. Then they discovered*
*they were and my twin brothers were born. So*
*now I wonder if they wish they hadn't adopt-*
*ed me, because they always complain about*
*everything I do. I don't think I belong in my*
*family. It is making me very miserable and I*
*am thinking of leaving home.*
                    *Unwanted, Partridge Cove*

Then we folded up the letters, exchanged them,
and wrote answers.

I wrote:

*Dear Unhappy,*
*You have two separate problems here.*
*First, about the kids who say you're weird.*
*You wouldn't want them for friends any-*
*way.*

*Secondly about the dog. I'm sure the*
*library must have some books on various*
*breeds of dogs. Take them out and try to find*
*a breed that would suit both your mother and*

*her partner. Maybe they could get a small dog that barks a lot. Or they could get a dog that would live in a kennel outside the house. If they can't agree on a dog, then they should consider getting a security system.*

*Aunt Partridge*

Jenny wrote:

*Dear Unwanted,*
*1) Your parents must have wanted you or they wouldn't have gone to the trouble of adopting you. It seems to me, if anybody was not wanted it was your twin brothers, because they didn't plan on having them.*
*2) You can't leave home until you are old enough to get a job and support yourself. So you may as well hang in there and make the best of it. You could try living with another family for a while. That might make you realize that your own family is the one you fit in best with.*

*Aunt Partridge*

"Hey, Ellen, that's pretty good," Jenny said. "I wonder why I didn't think of that myself. There's lots of dogs that Mom likes. She's always petting corgis and poodles when she sees them."

"Your letter was pretty good, too," I said. "It's true I probably wouldn't fit in with another family."

"You know," Jenny said, "we couldn't put these letters in the paper. Everybody would know who wrote them."

"You're right," I said. "Too bad."

"I'm glad we wrote them, though," Jenny said. "Writing things down makes you feel better."

We did feel better. We cheered up and started talking about the paper. Then Jenny said she had to go home. Anne was making pizza for supper because it was Cathy's favorite.

"I'll tell them your idea about the dog," she said.

Jenny always makes me feel better about myself, but I didn't feel better for long. When I went back to the house I found a note propped up on the table. It said, *Ellen would you do a white wash and wash a bunch of spinach.* No "please" or "thanks."

I dragged the hamper across the laundry room, tipped the clothes into the machine and dumped the detergent on top without measuring it. I spotted a pair of red socks mixed in with the white clothes but I didn't bother to take them out. Serves them all right if their stuff turns pink, I thought.

It was while I was washing the spinach that a

thought hit me. There was hardly any detergent left even though we'd just got a new box. Maybe Mrs. T. used more soap than we did, because our clothes were always a lot brighter when she washed them.

Then I had another thought. Suppose someone else had used the soap, and suppose they hadn't used it for washing clothes.

It was such an awful idea that I turned off the tap and just stared out the window.

Just then Dad came in and started talking to me.

"Oh, Ellen," he said. "Thanks for doing the spinach. I asked Mrs. T. to leave it for you to wash because you do such a careful job. Nobody else seems to get all the grit off the leaves. I don't know how you do it."

"Well, you have to wash each leaf separately," I said.

I felt bad about the red socks in the white wash.

# 14
# CONVERSATIONS

THE PERSON I REALLY wanted to talk to was Nerissa, because she always listened to me very seriously. So I went over to Satis Lodge and started digging moss out of the stone wall, and it wasn't long before she came out. As usual, I heard her voice before I saw her.

"I've been enjoying your newspaper enormously," she said. "I'm looking forward to the next issue."

"There might not be a next issue," I said. "My life's changed and I'm thinking of leaving home."

"You are?" she said. "And why is that?" She didn't sound as shocked as I thought she would.

"Well, for one thing, I don't really belong in that family," I said. "I've found out they adopted me."

"Ah!" said Nerissa. "You found that out just now?"

"Yes," I said. "Mum and Dad told me on Sunday, and it explains a lot. Like how they treat me more like a servant, while the twins get to do whatever they want. So I want to leave."

"I left home when I was very young," Nerissa said.

"You did?" I said. "Why?"

"For much the same reasons you've given."

"Did you find out you were adopted?"

"No, I wasn't adopted. But you can be born into a family and still feel that you don't belong to it. It's a sad fact of life that we can choose our friends, but we can't choose our families."

"The government should pass a law to change that."

"Meanwhile, we have to make the best of it," she said.

"But you didn't make the best of it. You ran away."

"Well, I tried," she said. "At the time, I hated every single person in my family. I'd seen gypsies camping out in the countryside where I lived, and their life looked a lot better than mine — sleeping under the stars, cooking outdoors on an open fire, eating meals sitting on the ground. I thought life with them would be a constant picnic. So I decided to pack up my things and join them."

"Did you have a suitcase?"

"I didn't think a suitcase would be appropriate for the kind of life I had in mind. I found a red checkered tablecloth, and then I gathered up some food — a pot of jam, a loaf of bread, fruit. And my lion."

"Your lion?"

"Yes, I remember that particularly because the worst part of the whole episode was that I lost my lion. I had an old stuffed one that I took to bed with me every night. I knotted everything up in the tablecloth, tied it to the end of a stick, put it over my shoulder, and went off to join the raggle-taggle gypsies, O!"

"What happened? Did you live with them?"

"No. I'm afraid it was very anti-climactic. These particular gypsies, when I saw them close up, were not very nice or very kind. They weren't as pleased to see me as I expected, and they took all my things, disappeared and left me alone. It began to get dark and I was terribly frightened."

"And then what happened?"

"Luckily I wasn't very far from home, and one of the stable boys came riding by. He lifted me up onto his saddle and took me home. And I was very glad to be back."

"But your family hadn't changed, had it?"

"Not at all. But my little escapade made me feel better about them — for a while, at least. One problem with families is that there are too many people crammed together in too small a space, and it's impossible to do anything without rubbing up against them…"

"But you said you had a lot of space — acres and acres?"

"True, but it was still hard to get away from people in the house. There were aunts and uncles everywhere, and some very unpleasant cousins. Yet my little stolen holiday among the unfriendly gypsies, short as it was, made me see my family in a different light."

"And so you never ran away again?"

"Oh, yes, I ran away eventually. There comes a moment in all our lives when we are ready to go out into the world. But if we go too soon, we leave part of ourselves behind, and we have a wound that never heals. We have to wait for the right moment."

I wanted to ask how you could tell when the right time came, but Nerissa was getting dreamy again.

"That's funny. I haven't thought about my little adventure with the gypsies in years," she said, and she turned and went off without saying goodbye.

I thought it was weird that she went back home so soon after she ran off to join the gypsies. I was sure that once I got away, I wouldn't go back, even if Mum and Dad went down on their hands and knees and begged me to.

I was just getting back to the weeding when Nerissa came down the path again and sat on a rock nearby.

"I've been thinking, Ellen," she said, "about what you said about not belonging."

"That's right," I said. "Mum and Dad have each other, and Timmy and Toby have each other. But I'm all by myself, like the cheese that stands alone."

"The cheese that stands alone?"

"You know, in the song — 'The Farmer in the Dell'?"

"Ah, yes, the song. You know, Ellen, I think we are a lot alike, you and I."

Just then I heard a car pull up at the gate, and saw that Mr. Clipper had arrived with a box, even though it wasn't Wednesday.

"Ellen, I'm afraid I have to go now," Nerissa said, "but we must speak of these things again. Do come back tomorrow if you can."

It was annoying that she left before I had time to

tell her about my other reason for wanting to leave home — and that was the awful suspicion I had about Timmy and the detergent. So I packed up my basket of tools and went home.

When I went inside, I saw that Dad's study door was slightly open. Usually he's sitting at his computer. This time he wasn't, so I stopped and peeped inside. He was sitting in his big chair, but he wasn't reading. He was holding his head in his hands.

We aren't supposed to disturb him when he's in his study unless it's something important that can't wait, but I pushed the door open a bit more and stood in the doorway.

"Dad," I said. "Can I come in?"

"Ellen?" he said. "Just the person I need to talk to. Come in and close the door."

"Is anything wrong?"

"Very wrong." He was talking quietly, so I sat down on the stool by his chair.

"Is it Mum?"

"No, no," he said. "It's something else. I've just had a very strange phone call from Cathy. She seems to think Timmy might know something about the vandalism that's happening in the village."

I didn't say anything but I guess the look on my face showed what I felt.

"How long have you known about this, Ellen?"

"Well, I first thought about it when Mrs. T. told us that the Lord sees the little sparrow fall, and even knows the number of hairs on everybody's head. Timmy looked very scared, like he did last summer. You know how he looks when he's scared — his skin gets pale and his freckles get dark. And I thought, 'Boy, you must really have a guilty conscience!'"

"He may well have a guilty conscience, Ellen, but that's not exactly proof that he's responsible for the vandalism."

"No, but there were other things, like the pruning clippers. They disappeared from the hook in the garden room. I looked everywhere, and then suddenly they were back on the hook. And it was about the time the maple tree was cut down at the bus stop. It was weird. But the thing that convinced me was the detergent by the washing machine. We had a full box not long ago, and yesterday I noticed it was nearly empty."

"Cathy said that just before the fish incident, she ran into Tim carrying a bag of powder, but he told her it was bone meal that Mrs. T. sent him out to buy."

"He lied?"

"Apparently, he did," Dad said. "Why would he

have done such a thing? Could it have anything to do with the events of last summer, or is it something else? What do you make of it, Ellen?"

"Well, he's the smallest one in the family," I said, "and he has trouble reading, and he doesn't do well in school. Nobody takes him seriously or treats him as if he's important, except for Mrs. T. who sticks up for him all the time. When he says something, we laugh at him. At least I do. So he gets more attention when he's being rude and difficult."

"You know, Ellen, I think you may be right," Dad said. "Tim probably feels like the odd man out in this family. Though, of course, that's no excuse for what he's done."

"Will he go to jail?" I said.

"He's too young for that, but he may well be charged in juvenile court. It isn't just the fish pond and the maple tree. There are other things — a stop sign pushed over at the intersection of Partridge Road and Seaview. That could have had very serious consequences. And someone has been tipping over mailboxes and throwing rocks at the lights in front of the motel."

"So his name and picture will be in the papers and everybody will know about it?"

"Well, he's under age, and they aren't allowed to print the names of young offenders. But it's impossible to keep something like this a secret for long. But no one will know for a day or two at least, and I need to think about it some more before we tell Mum. So let's just keep it between ourselves for the moment, Ellen."

I knew it was only a question of time before it was the talk of the village, and our family would be disgraced. Mrs. T. would say this was what happened when people didn't go to church and teach their children the Ten Commandments. Mrs. Banks would blame our parents for not giving us enough chores to keep us out of mischief, Mr. Weeks would blame Dad for not being strict enough, and Miss Jane Green would blame the teachers at school. Some would say Dad had no right to be teaching students down at the university when he couldn't even keep his own kids in order.

So everyone would know what Timmy had done, even if it didn't get written up in the paper.

# 15
## AN EDITORIAL

THE DAYS BEFORE THE NEWS got out that Tim was the Partridge Cove vandal were bad ones for Dad and me, and we had a lot of private conversations in his study. Dad was afraid that Mum would worry herself sick when she found out. He said it would be best if Gran never found out about Tim because that would upset Mum even more. I was afraid that all our neighbors would take it out on me, and maybe cancel their subscriptions to the paper.

What I discovered was that if you dread something very much for a long time, it's a relief when it actually happens. I also learned that sometimes it's not as bad as you expect, and that you can never tell ahead of time how people are going to react.

Mum was upset at first, but Dad said the main thing was to make Timmy understand the seriousness of his actions. He said Timmy should not only apologize, but do things to show people he was sorry. Mum suggested he plant another maple tree to replace the one he destroyed, and take the responsibility for looking after it. He should also offer to weed the flowerbeds in the village for the rest of the summer. Dad said he thought that was a good idea.

None of our neighbors seemed mad at me, and they weren't even mad at Timmy. It was really peculiar.

Mrs. Fenwick said she didn't believe a word of what she heard about Tim because he was always polite to her. She said the police were always making mistakes. The papers were full of examples.

"Don't tell Mrs. Banks I said that," she said. "The police can do no wrong in her eyes."

"But Timmy admitted that he did it," I said.

"The police sometimes bully people into making false confessions."

"Cathy didn't bully him."

"Well, all I can say is, I hope you're not being too hard on your little brother, Ellen. We all make mistakes."

Nerissa didn't hear any of the rumors, but I

ended up telling her all about Timmy, just like I told her about everything that happened in our lives. She said she knew a little boy once — a sort of brother — who always caused trouble. He was cruel to animals and little kids, and he got so bad that his parents finally sent him away to a special school.

"Did that cure him?"

"No. Nothing could cure him. He just got worse and worse as he got older…"

"What happened to him in the end?" I was very curious about this little kid who was like a brother to Nerissa, but she had got dreamy again and just got up and walked away to the house.

The most surprising thing of all was that Mrs. T. took Timmy's side. When she heard what he'd done, she just said there was more rejoicing in the Kingdom of Heaven over one person who sinned and repented than there was over all the people who hadn't done anything wrong in the first place.

"That's not fair," I said.

"If a man has a hundred sheep and one of them goes astray," she said, "he leaves the ninety-nine and goes into the wilderness looking for it. And when he finds the lost sheep, he calls his neighbors together and says, 'Rejoice with me because I have found the sheep that was lost.'"

"Well," I said, "Timmy didn't get lost, he did some awful things, and he's going to get punished. Dad's going to make him plant a maple tree at the bus stop, and weed all the public flowerbeds in the village for the rest of the summer. He'll have to buy the tree out of his own money, and he won't get paid for the weeding."

Then Mrs. T. told another story about a son that ran away from home and did bad things, and when he came home his dad killed a fat calf and threw a big party.

It's hopeless trying to argue with Mrs. T. because she just keeps quoting the Bible at you, so I decided to go and work on our paper. Finding out who the vandal was and having long talks with Dad about him had given me a lot of ideas for my next editorial. I even had a headline. I called it THE BLAME GAME, and this is what I wrote:

*There has been a lot of vandalism in Partridge Cove during the past weeks. A fish pond and a maple tree have been vandalized, and a stop sign has been torn down.*

*Many of us thought that summer visitors from the city or biker gangs were to blame. We were on the look-out for strangers who were acting suspiciously.*

*Some people blamed the schools for not teaching students to respect property, or television programs for encouraging violent behavior, or the government and the police for not catching criminals and keeping them in jail.*

*It is always easy to blame other people when things go wrong. It lets us be lazy and not do anything about it ourselves. But often the trouble starts at home and with ourselves. As you drive along the road to Partridge Cove, the view is spoiled by ugly signs advertising FISH AND CHIPS and HOT DOGS. And litter is seen all over the village. We should look in the mirror. We might discover that we are setting a bad example, and even causing the vandalism ourselves.*

Jenny thought the editorial was okay, but she couldn't think of a way to illustrate it, so we just faxed it to Higg. It came back almost immediately and he said he liked it very much.

*Ellen and Jenny,*
*This is an excellent editorial. It does what a good editorial should do. It describes and explains a situation. Then it takes a position*

*and expresses an opinion. It is both informa-
tive and thought-provoking.*

When the paper came out, we got a lot of posi-
tive feedback from the neighbors. Mrs. Fenwick
said she hoped it would lead people to question
their own behavior.

"I think you made a good point in your editorial, Ellen," Mrs. Banks said. "I was just telling Bill
this morning that I think he's partly to blame for
Tim's being so naughty. He's always telling the
twins about the pranks he got up to when he was
their age."

"Boys will be boys," Mr. Banks said. "But these
days they get the doctors and psychology guys on
their case, and say they have syndromes and disor-
ders and need to take medication. That's why
there's always a line-up at the drugstore. I had to
wait half an hour yesterday for my blood-pressure
pills. If you ask me, it's all a bunch of bull —"

"Nobody's asking you," Mrs. Banks said. "You'd
better read what Ellen wrote in her paper, and pay
attention to what she says."

# 16
# REVELATIONS

"ELLEN," DAD SAID SOON afterwards, "Cathy's coming over to have a word with me about this business with Tim. There's no need to bother Mum with it, and I wonder if we could use Somecot. It would be quieter down there, and we wouldn't be disturbed."

"Good idea," I said. It was Mrs. T.'s day to clean the living room, and I thought that when Cathy rang the bell we could take her down the garden to Somecot instead of inviting her into the house.

But there was so much noise from Mrs. T.'s vacuum cleaner that we didn't hear the bell. The door wasn't locked so Cathy just walked into the living room.

I was quite worried when I saw her because I

knew how Mrs. T. felt about Anne and Cathy living together. But I figured she wouldn't be rude to Cathy, especially when she was in her RCMP uniform.

At first the vacuum cleaner was roaring away so loudly that Mrs. T. didn't even notice Cathy. Then she looked around and saw her. She switched off the machine, and they stared at each other for a long time. Cathy looked almost as amazed to see Mrs. T. as Mrs. T. was to see her. Mrs. T. turned paler than usual, and got a sort of scared expression on her face. She looked as if she wanted to run out of the room, but Cathy was standing by one door, and Dad was in front of the other.

"So this is where you are," Cathy said after a while. "We've been wondering where you got to."

"I haven't done anything wrong," Mrs. T. said. "I've been here all the time. The professor'll tell you that."

"Would someone kindly explain what's going on," Dad said.

"This woman — I believe she now calls herself Mrs. T. — has a long criminal record," Cathy said. "Breaking and entering, shoplifting, telephone fraud. We've been wanting to talk to her about a hold-up in a bank, and a B & E in a B & B."

"I've never done banks," Mrs. T. said, "and I'm too old now for second-story jobs."

"I think this must be a case of mistaken identity, Cathy," Dad said. "I can vouch personally for Mrs. T. as an honest, hard-working person, whose moral standards are rather more strict than most people's. She's a very devout Christian."

"Oh, she's given you the religious line, has she?" Cathy said. "That's one of her specialties. Going door to door with a Bible and religious pamphlets in one hand and lock-picking equipment in the other. She carried out one hoist in a nun's outfit."

"Is this true?" Dad asked Mrs. T.

"I've put all that behind me now. I've done my time, and I want to go straight," Mrs. T. said. "I haven't done anything wrong while I've been here, have I?"

"No, indeed," Dad said. "But I don't understand. All those things you told us — about the Reverend and the children you fostered? None of that was true? Do you belong to a church at all?"

"There was a reverend," Mrs. T. said, sitting down. "I was in his home with half a dozen other foster kids. I was the oldest and I worked hard raising those kids. I had no choice. That man was the meanest man on earth. He'd eat a whole chicken for his dinner while us kids had a bowl of what they called soup. Mostly water with a few vegetables floating in it. No kid ever got a scrap of that chicken.

He'd eat it watching our faces. And ask us if it smelled good. It perked up his appetite. And on Sunday he'd be in the pulpit preaching. 'Suffer the little children to come unto me' and 'Whosoever hurts the foot of one of the least of my children, he does it unto me.' Everybody thought he was a saint, fostering all those kids. Not that he did much fostering. It was his wife and me that did all the scrubbing and cleaning. But one thing he did do was hammer the Bible into us. We had to listen to it morning, noon and night and recite it back to him. He made us learn bits off by heart every day. More if he said we'd done something wrong."

"I see," Dad said.

"He was the biggest hypocrite in the world. And nobody believed us kids — not the neighbors or the teachers or the social workers. We had no mums and dads looking out for us. He was a reverend, and they treated him like he was God Almighty. So I learned from day one that religion was the ticket. If you had it, you could do what you wanted and get away with it. Same in the pen..."

"The pen?"

"The penitentiary. You say you're born again, the chaplain gets the credit, and you're out on parole. Works like a charm. With the judge, too. Everybody thinks you're rehabilitated. When you get out, though, it's not easy. It's tough finding a job. You've got no references, for one thing. I heard someone talk about this job. A professor they said, and nutty as a fruitcake. No offense, Professor."

"None taken, Mrs. T."

"Anyway, I thought it would suit me just fine here," Mrs. T. went on. "Kids, a sick wife, cleaning, cooking. I'm used to hard work like I said. The religion, well, I thought it would make a good impression, make up for having no references."

"I have no quarrel with Mrs. T.'s explanation, Cathy," Dad said, "and I have no objection to her remaining with us."

"You want to take that risk?" Cathy said.

"What risk?" Mrs. T. said. "They don't have anything anybody would want to steal. Only a lot of old books and junk."

Just then Cathy's cellphone rang, and she listened and told whoever called that she'd be right there.

"Look, I have to go now," Cathy said, "but we'll want to talk to Mrs. T. down at the station about those two matters I mentioned."

"I'll be very glad to accompany her and vouch for her character," Dad said. "They're getting quite used to seeing me down at the police station. The superintendent now greets me like an old friend."

He walked Cathy to the door and saw her out.

"Mrs. T.," I said, "when you said you didn't want to meet Cathy and Anne and Jenny, it was just because you were afraid Cathy would recognize you, wasn't it?"

"I didn't want that girl drawing pictures of me," Mrs. T. said. "I still don't want her drawing me."

"So you don't mind Jenny coming in as long as she doesn't sketch you?" I said. Just then Dad came back.

"I guess I'd better get the lunch on," Mrs. T. said.

"Not quite so fast, Mrs. T.," Dad said. "Now that Cathy's gone I do have some questions of my own. All those appliances and gadgets you've been bringing in. I think I need some clarification about their acquisition. I am assuming that they were not the lucky finds at church fairs and garage sales that we were led to believe."

"Well, it took a bit of luck to get them," Mrs. T. said. "And where they came from they had a lot more stuff than you, and could afford to buy more. See, it's like this, Professor. As soon as I walked in that door, I could see you had no street smarts…"

"Now, just one minute, Mrs. T.," Dad said, "The economic status of the owners of those appliances is totally irrelevant. The fact is that my kitchen is full of stolen goods. That makes me a thief."

"More like a fence, Professor, but…"

"Mrs. T., those appliances must be returned to their rightful owners."

"Can't do that," said Mrs. T. "They're all used anyway. They wouldn't want them back, and those that came from stores, they couldn't sell them anyways."

"We could take them to the Salvation Army," I said. "But can't we keep the night-light? Timmy won't go to sleep without it."

"This gets more and more complicated," Dad said, taking out his handkerchief and wiping his forehead. "It will take a lot of sorting out. Perhaps you're right, Mrs. T., we should get lunch on the table." That seemed to make him think of something else.

"Mrs. T., that garden of yours that has been supplying so much of our food. Do you even have a garden?" Mrs. T. looked as if she was about to start another explanation, but Dad just held up his hand.

"Never mind, never mind," he said. "We can discuss this later. Ellen, not a word about any of this to the others." Then he went to the fridge and got a can of beer.

"Drinking in the middle of the day?" Mum said when she came to the table.

"Mrs. T., you forgot to say grace," Tim said.

Mrs. T. bowed her head in prayer, and Dad drank half his glass of beer in one gulp.

"Wonderful tomatoes," Mum said. "How do you do it, Mrs. T.? Do you have a greenhouse?"

"I don't have a greenhouse myself," Mrs. T. said, "but my neighbors do. And they grow a lot more stuff than they can eat."

Dad took another big gulp of his beer.

# 17
# CALM WEATHER

FOR A WHILE THAT summer it seemed as if nothing would ever be the same again. Mum and Dad told me I was adopted, we discovered that Timmy was the Partridge Cove vandal, and it turned out that Mrs. T. was an ex-convict. Then, as suddenly as all the shocks happened, and we had just got used to them, they faded into the background, and things got back to normal. It was a bit like a sea mist that comes down and muffles everything so that you can't see any of the regular trees and buildings, and then it suddenly lifts and leaves the garden exactly as it was before.

Except that nothing was really like it was before. There were a lot of small changes, some of them good, and some bad. At lunch we now had a moment of silence before we started to eat. We stared at our plates for a while and listened to each other's stomachs rumbling.

"This is a new development," Gran said when she came up for her Sunday visit. "I thought nobody bothered to say grace in this household."

"A moment of quiet reflection before embarking on our meal doesn't do anybody any harm," Dad said. "In fact, it helps the digestion."

"I liked hearing Mrs. T. talk to the Lord," Timmy said, "but they're not talking to each other anymore."

"If you have a stomach problem," Gran said, "I can suggest a very good product I've seen advertised on TV. It comes recommended by a lot of doctors."

The fallacy of appealing to authority, I thought, but I kept quiet.

"If you're taking all the stuff you see advertised on TV," Mum said, "you probably need a doctor for your head, not your stomach."

"Perhaps Gran would like more vegetables," Dad said.

"The carrots are not very good, I'm afraid," Mum said.

"Perhaps Mrs. T. has been neglecting her garden," Gran said. "The vegetables don't seem quite as fresh as they were before."

"Well, it's late in the season," Dad said, "and it's been very dry."

"I hear Timmy has been watering the flower beds in the village," Gran said. "I approve of volunteer work…"

"Quite right, Mother," Dad said quickly, "and you were also right when you said that it's quicker in the long run to do jobs by hand."

"I noticed that the electrical gadgets have outlived their usefulness," she said, looking at the spaces in the kitchen where the mixer, the grater and the blender had been.

"Mrs. T. took them to the Salvation Army," I said.

"She did?" Gran said. "I wish you'd asked me first. That blender could have come in handy when I make dips for my bridge group."

"Well, it's advertised on TV," Mum said. "Just call the toll-free number. They'll probably throw in some indigestion medicine for free."

Usually Gran ignores Mum when she's being rude, but sometimes Mum goes too far, and Gran's feelings get hurt. It was giving me indigestion wondering if Mum would go too far.

Later, I asked Dad why Mum was grouchy.

"I think Mum was tense because she was afraid that Gran would find out about Timmy."

One good thing was that Jenny now came for lunch or dinner whenever she wanted. We told Jenny that Mrs. T. had no problem with Anne and Cathy living together, but she was afraid of being photographed and sketched.

Mrs. T. also stopped arguing with Dad, and she started asking him questions instead. She asked him about the arguments for the existence of God, and what a humanist is.

"We believe that the solutions to problems lie in our own actions rather than in divine intervention," he said. "And we think good deeds should be based on understanding and concern for others, not on fear of punishment by a supernatural being."

"I sure wish I'd known all this when I was living with the Reverend," Mrs. T. said, "and when I was talking to the chaplain at the…last place I worked in."

"I can lend you an excellent book on the subject," Dad said. "I'll mark certain passages so you won't have to read the whole thing."

"Won't do me any good, Professor."

"I see," Dad said. "Quite. Well, I have no objection to going over the arguments as often as you wish. And, if you get tired of listening to me, you can get Ellen to explain them."

"Why won't Mrs. T. borrow your books?" I asked Dad one day, after I'd explained what begging the question meant three times.

"Because Mrs. T. has never learned to read and write." Dad said that he and Mum were trying to think of a way to help her with it. He said I shouldn't mention it to the twins or let her know that I'd noticed, because it was a great embarrassment for her.

So much was going on at home that I practically forgot about being adopted. So I was surprised when Nerissa asked me if I was still planning to leave home.

"Oh, no," I said. "I don't think I'm ready just now. Maybe later."

"What made you postpone your plans?" she said.

"Dad needs me," I said. "He wouldn't be able to manage without me, because we have a lot of problems in our family at the moment."

"But you have a housekeeper, don't you?"

"Well, Mrs. T. is part of the problem," I said. I hadn't meant to tell Nerissa about Mrs. T. being in prison, but she asked so many questions that somehow it all came out, and I ended up telling her the whole story. She was very interested.

"So you see," I said, "Dad needs someone to talk

to and ask for advice, when he doesn't want to bother Mum with things."

"And what else has he been needing advice about lately?" she said.

"Timmy, mainly," I said. "We've been trying to think of ways to keep him out of trouble and give him a sense of responsibility."

"And does Timmy have any ideas of his own about that?"

"He wants to join a church and become an altar boy or a choir boy."

"And how are you and Jenny coming along with your newspaper work?" she said.

"Jenny's fine," I said. "Her mum and Cathy are getting two schnauzers, and Jenny and I are going to pick names for them. We thought of calling them Romulus and Remus, only one's a boy and one's a girl. And I'm writing an article on choosing the right breed of dog. Then I'm thinking of writing one on choosing the right name for a dog."

One of the things that had happened lately was that I seemed to have no trouble thinking up ideas for articles and editorials, and writing about them. Apart from the articles on dogs, I wanted to write about television commercials and how we shouldn't be taken in by them, and about the treatment of criminals and how they should be encouraged and given interesting projects to do rather than being punished, and about the dangers of using pesticides, and about not letting people own guns.

"Well, Ellen, I'd like to read all the future issues of your newspaper," Nerissa said.

Her tone of voice surprised me, though I didn't know exactly why.

After I went home, I thought that was the first time she hadn't walked off in the middle of a conversation. Our talk had ended the way talks with friends usually end, with people saying things like "See you later" and "Nice talking to you."

"It's always good to talk to you, Ellen," she said. "I can't tell you how much I've looked forward to these conversations of ours. I've enjoyed them so much. I almost feel like a member of your family because you've told me so much about them."

"I like our talks, too," I said. I was going to say that I felt like a member of her family, but then I realized that I really didn't know much about her at all.

Jenny was right when she said that Nerissa asked me way more questions than I asked her.

# 18
# FINAL INTERVIEW

I WENT OVER TO Satis Lodge the next day as soon
as I'd finished helping Mrs. Fenwick with the flower
boxes on her deck. But instead of creeping up on
me the way she usually did, Nerissa came hurrying
out to the garden as soon as I got there, as if she
had been looking out for me.

"Ellen," she said, "do you remember when you
told me there were no rich and famous people in
Partridge Cove?"

"Yes," I said.

"Well, you were wrong."

"You mean you?" I said, because she had a
funny kind of smile on her face. "Are you rich and
famous?"

"Perhaps not so rich," she said. "In fact, not

really rich at all, comparatively speaking, but fairly famous."

"Are you a movie star?"

"Film stars aren't the only famous people in the world," she said. "But you've told me so much about yourself that I've decided to tell you about my own life. I'm going to let you interview me. So why don't you run and get the little cassette recorder you use for interviews."

"Could we do it tomorrow?" I said. "You're supposed to plan the questions ahead of time and make out a list of them before you do an interview."

"I have time on my hands just now," she said, "and I'm afraid I might change my mind if we wait until tomorrow. Don't worry about the questions. I'm sure you'll be able to think of something. And if you can't, I'll help you out."

"Where will we do the interview?" I said.

"Why not do it right here in the garden where we've had so many of our talks?"

So I went home and gave my hands a good scrubbing. Then I found my notebook and pencil and got Mum's cassette player.

When I went back, Nerissa was sitting in a chair she'd carried from the porch and set in the shade. She'd taken off her hat and her dark glasses so I could see her face for the first time. It was a very beautiful face, with light skin and big gray eyes, and her hair was long and silvery. I set my cassette player on a rock, turned it on and sat down on the grass.

"First of all I think I should tell you the name most people know me by," she said. "That name is Nina Kay."

"I thought your name was Nerissa."

"That's the name I have when I'm talking to you."

"But you can't have a different name for everyone you talk to," I said.

Then she started talking before I had time to ask anything else. As she talked, she looked out at the sea, and soon she seemed to forget I was there. It was as if she was talking to herself or thinking aloud.

"I was born in a small town in Australia," she said. "It was far from any city. There were very few people in the town, and most of them were farmers and their families. It was understood that most of us would become farmers or farmers' wives. But at a very early age, I decided to become a writer. I knew what I wanted to be, but I had no idea how to go about it. It seemed an impossible dream for someone living in the heart of the country, and unable to go to school, or to college."

"Did you have a lot of books at home or in the library?" I asked.

"No," she said, "no books. And there was no library in the town. There were newspapers, and occasionally magazines and journals came our way."

"If you didn't go to school and you didn't have any books, how did you learn anything?"

"What?" she said, as if she was surprised to find someone there listening to her. "How did we learn? We did correspondence courses. Packages of lessons were sent to us through the mail, and we worked on them at the kitchen table. It was a very haphazard process."

"But you couldn't become a writer if you never went to school."

"Well, I did," she said. "I became a very successful writer, but in a very roundabout way."

"How did you do it?"

"By leaving home. I left home when I was only a few years older than you. One day I saw in the paper that a ship sailing from Australia to England was advertising for waiters, kitchen help and chambermaids. I applied for the job, lying about my age, and they hired me. When I got to England, I had very little money — only what I'd saved from my earnings on the ship, and from the tips given to me by rich passengers. But with that money I was able to rent a tiny attic room in a London square. It was not very comfortable, but I had a wonderful library nearby, where I spent a lot of my time. And that was when I wrote my first book."

"What was it about?" I said.

"It was about all the people whose rooms I'd cleaned on the ship," she said. "There were many people from all different countries, and every night when I got back to my bunk, no matter how tired I was, I wrote down in my diary everything that I'd seen and heard. This helped me to recall the voyage very vividly. There happened to be a publishing house in the square where I lived, so I took my novel there. I was worried because I wasn't very good at spelling and grammar, but I was lucky. One of the editors read my book, liked it, and published it. When it appeared, a great many people read it and liked it, and clamored for more books by me. And so, I kept on writing."

"Did you always stay in the same attic?"

"No. I didn't... There were certain difficulties, and I moved away. I moved very often, from one country to another."

"Weren't you lonely?"

"Not as long as I was at my desk writing. A writer's desk is not a lonely place. In fact, it is the least lonely place in the world. I had my work and, in spite of my unsettled life, I was happy for many years. But I began to have difficulty with my writing. I was trying to write a book about my own childhood, and my own past. And suddenly, I lost all pleasure in writing. Then I began to doubt the value of anything I'd written, and I got to the point where I could no longer write at all."

"You had writer's block," I said. "All writers get that."

"What?" she said, looking startled.

"I got that last year when I was writing a book. Jenny helped me get over it."

"Ah, yes," she said. "Your good friend, Jenny. I had a good friend, too, and he helped me. He suggested that I leave the city where I was living with all its distractions and noise, and find a quiet place where I could breathe fresh air, and have solitude and peace, and where nobody would know who I was. So he looked around, and eventually he found Satis Lodge."

"And did the peace and fresh air cure your writer's block?"

"Those things helped. But something helped even more. I found someone who regularly brought me words and ideas that opened the door on the vanished world of my past, and gave me back the memory of my younger self. I remembered again what it is like to be young and confused, and I found a way of telling my story."

"And did you finish your book?"

"Yes, I did, Ellen," she said. "Once I got started, I was able to work very rapidly. I finished my book the day before yesterday."

"What's it called?" I asked.

"Ah, I haven't got a title yet. What would you call it, if you were me?"

I thought for a moment. "I'd call it *The Cheese Stands Alone*," I said. "You remember when we talked about how we felt different from other people?"

"I remember all our conversations, Ellen," she said. "And I think your suggestion's an excellent one."

Then she told me more about her life. She talked on and on, until we heard footsteps hurrying down the path. It was the man from Seattle. I was quite surprised to see him because it wasn't Wednesday.

"I've been confiding in Ellen," Nerissa said. "I've told her the story of my life. And in return she's given me a title for my book."

"Nessa!" he said. "Do you have any idea what time it is?"

"Ah, yes," she said, looking at her watch. "Time and tide and the Red Eye wait for no man."

"The Red Eye?" I said in alarm. "Where is he?"

"The Red Eye isn't a he," Nerissa said. "It's the overnight flight across the continent from the west coast to New York. Those who catch it arrive with red eyes, so I hear. I'm afraid the interview is at an end, Ellen."

"I'll write it up," I said, "and I'll let you read it before I put it in the paper, because I like to get everything right."

"I know you do, Ellen," she said. "I have perfect confidence in your work. Otherwise, I wouldn't have trusted you with the interview. Thank you for doing it."

Then she turned and walked up the path toward the house, leaning a little heavily on the arm of Mr. Clipper, as if she needed support.

# 19
# MORE REVELATIONS

I COULDN'T WAIT TO call Jenny and tell her about the interview, but when I got home, Dad asked me to help with supper. I grated some cheese for the top of the casserole and put it in the oven. Then I set the table.

I only started thinking about the interview again when we were eating the casserole.

"Did you ever hear of a writer called Nina Kay?" I asked Mum and Dad.

"Of course," Mum said. "Everyone's heard of Nina Kay. I have all her books. She wrote her first one when she was very young — still a teenager, I believe. It was called *Maiden Voyage*, about a lot of people on a ship."

"Well, that's who our mysterious neighbor is," I said.

"Whatever makes you think that?"

"She told me herself this afternoon. She let me interview her, and she told me all about her life."

"That doesn't sound like Nina Kay," Mum said. "She never gives interviews. I've heard that she comes from a very aristocratic and titled family, and doesn't want to embarrass them with her books."

"Is her picture on the books?" Dad asked.

"Oh, no," Mum said. "She refuses to let people take her photograph. Her book jackets are very unusual — plain white covers with no design. And I believe even her name is a pseudonym."

"What's a pseudonym?" said Timmy.

"It's the name that writers use when they don't want to put their own names on their books."

"But how strange that she told Ellen that was her name," Dad said.

"If it was, I'd love to meet her," Mum said.

"Well, you can't," Toby said, "because she's gone away."

"Gone away?"

"Yes," said Toby. "We saw her getting into the water taxi with the other lady and a lot of suitcases, and then the man put a lot of boxes in his car and drove away. The house is empty and they've gone for good."

"That's easy to check out," Dad said. "We can give John Linton a call. The real estate office will be closed, but he won't mind if we call him at home."

"Do give him a call," Mum said. "Ellen's raised my curiosity."

So Dad called John Linton and said we were wondering if the house next door was empty again.

"It is," Dad said. "I see. Oh, no, we don't know of anyone interested in renting it. We just wondered if the last tenant left a forwarding address, because we'd like to contact her." He said "I see" several times and then hung up.

"Did you get her name and address?" Mum asked.

"He never knew it," Dad said. "The correspondence — the rent checks and damage deposit — came from a publishing house in New York. All the details were arranged by phone with someone in Seattle."

"That would be Mr. Clipper," I said. "I was right when I thought he was picking up the work she'd done. Only it wasn't sewing. It was writing."

"Amazing!" Mum said.

"Isn't that something?" Dad said.

"If Ellen did that interview, it would be one of the rare interviews in existence. It would be of great interest to the literary world," Mum said, "not to mention some of the big publications."

"Perhaps we should listen to it," Dad said.

Just then the bell rang and it was Jenny.

"I thought you were going to come over this afternoon, Ellen," she said. So we filled her in on what had happened and what we'd learned about Nina Kay.

"You're just in time to listen to the interview with us," I said.

So I went and got the cassette player and put it on the coffee table, and we all huddled around to listen. It was very faint at first and I turned up the volume. Then Larry's voice came on because the tape was still in there from when I'd tried to interview him.

"Look here, Ellen," he said, "I don't mind telling you about how I came to work at the library and be a librarian. But as I've told you and Jenny many times before, I'm not going to discuss my love life with you. If you put stuff like that in your paper, I'd have the whole of Partridge Cove on my neck...so you'd better shut that thing off."

Then there was a click, and then another click. And then the voice of Nina Kay started. It sounded a bit different on tape from when I'd heard it in the garden. It was a beautiful voice, and Mum, who was sitting next to Dad on the sofa, held on to his arm, as if she was scared of what she might hear.

"First of all I think I should tell you the name most people know me by. That name is Nina Kay."

"I thought your name was Nerissa."

"That's the name I have when I'm talking to you."

Then there was a slight click and the voice stopped. Everyone looked at me as if they expected me to do something.

"Turn over the cassette, Ellen," Mum said.

"I...I didn't turn over the tape," I said.

"You didn't turn over the tape?"

"Didn't you hear it click when she was talking?" Dad said.

"No," I said. "I mean, maybe. I was listening so hard I forgot about the tape altogether. And then when Mr. Clipper came and interrupted us, and she went back to the house, I just picked up my stuff and came home."

"So you didn't record the interview at all," Dad said.

"Ellen, how could you be so careless?" Mum said. "What a tremendous loss!"

"Boy, you really screwed up," Toby said.

"Ellen blew it," Timmy said, and he rolled around on the floor, laughing.

"Oh, poor Ellen," Jenny said. "Can you remember what she said?"

"Yes, I think I can remember everything," I said. "It was so interesting."

"Then you should write down everything you remember as soon as possible," Mum said. "After all, people did interviews before they had tape recorders. It's late now, but you should do it first thing tomorrow morning."

"I'll never get to sleep if I'm worried about holding it in my mind till tomorrow," I said. "I'd better start right now."

"Maybe Ellen could go down to Somecot and write it there," Jenny said. "My sleeping bag's still down there and I could stay with her."

"Good idea," Dad said.

"So Ellen gets to stay up till midnight," Timmy said. "No fair."

"Take some milk and cookies, in case you get hungry," Mum said, and she started to pack up a picnic basket for us.

"You'd better watch out," Timmy shouted after us. "There's a lot of dangerous things prowling around down there in the dark — raccoons, and kidnappers, and rodents."

"Category error," I said, and we headed off down the garden to spend the night in Somecot. Jenny carried the basket, and I carried my notebooks and pencils.

# 20
# FAME

I WAS AWAKENED THE next morning by the creak of a door opening. At first I didn't know whether I was in my own room or in the bottom bunk at Jenny's. Then I realized I was in my sleeping bag on the floor in Somecot, and Jenny was coming in carefully balancing a tray with a jug of orange juice, a basket of muffins and a banana.

"It's really late, Ellen," she said. "You must have stayed up all night."

"I think it was after midnight," I said, as I grabbed one of the muffins. "The sky was full of stars."

"Mom brought these over," Jenny said. "Good grief, Ellen, you went to bed with all your clothes on." I ate another muffin and drank a glass of juice while Jenny thumbed through my notebook. "Wow, you've written pages and pages."

I was so tired I wanted to crawl back into my sleeping bag, but I needed to go to the bathroom. I was glad I'd gone to bed with my clothes on because I was much too tired to get dressed. So we walked up to the house.

"Have you got the notebook, Ellen?" Dad said. "I'll type up what you've written, and then I'd like to show it to a colleague of mine in the English department."

"I think you'd better take a shower and change into some clean clothes," Mum said.

I didn't want my writing shown to some English professor, and I didn't want to take a shower and change my clothes, but I was too tired to argue.

"I'm just going to have an after-breakfast nap," I said.

A few days later, Dad's colleague from the university came over to talk to me.

"There's no doubt in my mind," he said, "that your neighbor was Nina Kay." He told me that all the facts I'd found out about her life would lead to a better understanding of her work.

"But I don't want everyone to know the facts I found about her life," I said. "I don't want to be a paparazzo."

"Honey," he said, "it's very unlikely Nina Kay would have told you so much if she'd really intended to keep it a secret. She sent you to get your cassette player, and believed you were recording every word. My guess is that she'd already decided to give an interview before her next book came out. She probably intended to do that when she got back to New York. Then she met you, learned that you were editing a newspaper, and the idea of letting you do the interview appealed to her. Her books show that she has quite a sense of humor, and it would be a good joke."

"Why would it be a joke for me to do the interview?"

"Oh, I didn't mean to offend you," he said. "It's just that so many journals would have paid huge sums to interview her. The joke is on them."

I couldn't see that it was a joke, and I was annoyed that Dad had shown my interview to someone else without my permission.

Then two reporters from the mainland arrived and wanted to talk to me. They had people with them, and they went into the garden of Satis Lodge and took a lot of photographs. Then they took pictures of me and asked me a bunch of questions. I tried not to tell them very much. When they asked how tall she was, and how old, and what she wore,

I said, "medium height," "not an old lady and not a young one," and "a hat and sunglasses." When they asked what we talked about, I said she asked me about Partridge Cove and the people who live here.

When the papers came out, I read the same kinds of lies that had been printed about us the summer before. All the headlines were stupid:

### PARTRIDGE COVE LIKELY SETTING FOR FAMOUS WRITER'S NEXT BESTSELLER

*Residents of Partridge Cove were surprised to learn recently that one of their summer visitors was the bestselling author Nina Kay, often compared with Greta Garbo who guarded her privacy with the famous line "I want to be alone." Neighbors who spoke with Ms. Kay said she was a glamorous forty-some woman who concealed her identity with dark glasses and a broad-brimmed hat. Those who met her believed she was gathering material for her next novel. Since two of her novels have already been made into movies, it seems likely that the next blockbuster movie will be filmed in Partridge Cove.*

### MOVIE CREWS EXPECTED TO DISRUPT RURAL QUIET OF PARTRIDGE COVE

*The small seaside village of Partridge Cove will soon be preparing for an unusual influx of summer visitors as it is expected that a movie company will start work on the latest novel by Nina Kay, the famous author who spent the summer there gathering material. The president of the Chamber of Commerce said that the many bed and breakfast places in the area are well able to absorb the influx. When asked if they were suitable for Hollywood stars used to lavish accommodations, she said that most of the bed and breakfasts are "fit for royalty."*

"It's a good thing she won't read this junk," I said.

"I think she probably will," Mum said.

"She won't be able to buy these papers in New York," I said.

"Her publisher is sure to have a clipping service that picks up references to her in papers all around the world," Mum said.

"But she'll think I told all these stupid lies."

"She must have known that reporters would want to talk to you," Mum said. "And I think she understands better than most people how words get distorted in the papers."

"Maybe I should write letters to the editors and tell them that their reporters got everything wrong. The new book isn't a novel, and it isn't set in Partridge Cove, and it isn't going to be made into a movie. It's about her own life, and it takes place where she grew up in Australia."

"You could do that," Mum said, "but there's no guarantee that your letter would be printed. Papers don't publish too many letters to the editor suggesting their own reporters are unreliable. And if they *do* print corrections, they put them in small print in a part of the paper where they're not likely to catch readers' attention."

"Well, that's not fair," I said.

When a reporter from *The Colonial Times* drove up from the city to ask me some questions about Nina Kay, I told him I was disgusted by all the yellow journalism.

"Yellow journalism! Wow!" he said. "Tell me about it!"

"It's journalism that tries to get attention by exaggerating and being sensational," I said. "It's called that because of a paper in New York a long time ago that had a cartoon showing a girl in a yellow dress. I think it was the first time a color picture was used in a newspaper."

He talked to me for over an hour, and before he left he said that if, in a few more years, I still wanted to be a journalist, I should get in touch with him. He said they had an intern program for training young reporters at his paper.

When his article came out, it had a photograph of me in front of Dad's bookcase, looking like a stupid owl. The headline above the picture said:

*YOUNG WANNABE JOURNALIST*
*GETS MAJOR SCOOP*

The article said I ran a newspaper, and that I'd managed to talk Nina Kaye into giving me an exclusive interview for it. She had agreed to do it because she was grateful for all the gossip I'd passed on to her about my neighbors and other local people to use in her next novel.

"Now everybody's going to be mad at me, and think they'll end up in a novel," I said.

"Well, it doesn't matter if they cancel their subscriptions now," Jenny said, "because we only have one more issue to get out."

"Maybe the best thing is to write up a full and

truthful account of your meetings with her and put it in the *Partridge Inquirer*," Mum said. "Then readers will be able to judge for themselves which account is more truthful."

"Will Nerissa's clipping service pick up my paper?" I said.

"Probably not," Mum said, "but if you send it to the publishing house, it just might get passed on to her."

"I should do that anyway," I said, "because she's already paid for two subscriptions."

# 21
# ENDINGS

WE KEPT GETTING CALLS from reporters wanting to ask questions about Nina Kay, so Dad said
we should get an answering machine.

"Maybe Mrs. T. can find us one at a church sale,"
Timmy said. Mrs. T. said she'd be glad to look out
for one, but Dad said that wouldn't be necessary.
He went straight out and bought one, and it
worked pretty well. The only problem was that
Timmy kept calling from the courtesy telephone in
the supermarket and leaving messages saying he
wouldn't be home for supper because a UFO had
landed in Partridge Cove and it was taking him to
another planet. No such luck.

Once the excitement died down, Jenny and I
were able to concentrate on our last paper. It was a

good issue. I wrote a short editorial thanking all our subscribers and everyone who had helped us. There were lots of items for the Special Occasions column. Mrs. Fenwick got a new parrot and called it Boney. We put in Anne and Cathy's schnauzers named Romula and Remus. Higg had finished his poem about the maple tree that was vandalized. It was called "The Sapling," and he let us print it in our Arts section.

Most of the paper was taken up with the article Mum had suggested I write to set the record straight about Nina Kay. I told how she went into hiding and led a secretive life because she didn't want readers to know that she'd never been to school, and that she grew up in a small country place in Australia and had an Australian accent. She thought readers wouldn't take her seriously if they knew all that. So she wouldn't let her publisher put a photo on her books, or any personal information on the covers.

Then one reporter claimed to have learned from "an unnamed source" that she came from an aristocratic family with a castle in England or Scotland. That started a guessing game about who she was, and the mystery made people buy more of her books. Her publishers were happy, but she was afraid of what would happen when readers found out who she really was. So she went into hiding, moving from place to place, always terrified that someone would find out her true identity and let out the secret of her past. Then everyone would accuse her of lying to them on purpose.

But eventually she decided that all the secrecy had to stop. She was trying to decide which important journalist she would choose for the interview when she came to Satis Lodge. And that's how the *Partridge Inquirer* got its interview. I also said that the interview would be followed by a book that was different from all her others. It would be her own life story.

We ran off a few extra copies of the final issue, and Pat and Myra agreed to sell them for us at the bookstore. They sold so quickly that people left orders for even more copies.

We had plenty of money in the bank at the end of the summer, so Jenny and I decided to have lunch at the Creamery again, and split the rest between us to buy books and stuff for school.

The bookstore put all of Nina Kay's books in the window, and Larry and Miss Jane Green made a display of her books in the library. They said there was a waiting list of people who wanted to read them.

"I was quite impressed when I read about you in *The Colonial Times*, Ellen," Miss Jane Green said.

"Where did you learn all that information about yellow journalism?"

"Higg told us," I said.

"Well, he must be an excellent teacher," she said, "but you'd better not let him hear you calling him Higg."

"You know," Jenny said afterwards, when we were sitting outside Mrs. A.'s Candy Kitchen sampling the ice cream flavor of the week, "we're going to have to get used to calling Higg Mr. Higginson again."

"It'll seem weird saying, 'Hello, Mr. Higginson. How's Kennedy Worthington Russell getting along?'"

But we did get used to it. A few weeks into the school year, Miss Brodie, our teacher, said, "Ellen and Jenny, Mr. Higginson would like to speak with you in his classroom during recess."

"Hello, Mr. Higginson," we said. "How's Kennedy Worthington Russell getting along?"

"Oh, Thumper's fine. We've got him in daycare, and he's starting to talk. He can say a whole sentence. We think he's a genius."

"Gran says every child's a genius before he's ten," I said.

"What's the sentence?" Jenny said.

"Doggy bark. He can't say *b* yet, but that's what

we think he's trying to say. Anyway, I didn't call you in to tell you about Thumper's brilliant remarks. Something odd and interesting has happened. I got a call from a publisher in Seattle who's bringing out a literature textbook for college students. They want to use my poem 'The Sapling.'"

"Wow!" Jenny said. "That's awesome!"

"Will you get a lot of money for it?" I said.

"I'm not sure about the money, but it means a lot of exposure for me and my poetry. But I'm curious about how they found the poem. Do you suppose it has something to do with Nina Kay?"

"Maybe it has something to do with Mr. Clipper," I said. "He came from Seattle. I never did find out his real name. And Nerissa took out an extra subscription for a friend."

"When the poem is printed in the textbook," Higg said, "there'll be a note to say that it first appeared in *The Partridge Inquirer*. So you'll get some of the credit."

Gran always says that everything happens in threes. That makes Dad raise his eyebrows because it's a hasty generalization and it's not logical. All the same, three strange things did happen around the same time.

One day Dad came out of his study with his reading glasses on, holding the newspaper.

"Ellen," he said, "here's something that will interest you." It was a big headline:

### *MORE STARTLING REVELATIONS ABOUT THE MYSTERIOUS NINA KAY*

*The recent flurry of interest in the novelist Nina Kay continues to produce startling revelations. Researchers in Australia have now discovered that she started life as Agnes Skaggs, born to the unmarried daughter of a large sheep farm owner. A scholar at the University of Melbourne contacted a retired postmistress by telephone.*

*The postmistress said she remembered her well, and that the local children found her peculiar, and taunted her with the name "Aggie Skaggy." The postmistress recalled that she was always holed up in sheds about the place, with whatever stuff she could find to read, and often with an old stuffed toy. "We always wondered what happened to Aggie Skaggy," she said. "She disappeared suddenly one day. And about a year later, her mother disappeared as well."*

"This isn't true, is it?" I said.

"That's just what I was going to ask you," Dad said. "You were the one who knew her."

"I don't know. Maybe she'll write about it in her new book."

Pat said she'd already seen the new book advertised, and that she'd ordered several copies because a lot of local people were interested in it.

"It's called *The Cheese Stands Alone*," she said. "What a funny title! I wonder what it means."

The last thing that happened was the strangest of all. One evening Dad checked the answering machine, and there was a message from Mrs. T.

"Professor Fremedon," the voice said, "it's been good working for you and your missus and the kids but I won't be coming in anymore. Old habits are hard to break, and I'm too old to change my ways. Be a good boy, Timmy. Listen to what your dad says, and always clean your plate up."

"What does that mean?" I said.

"For one thing it means that we won't be seeing Mrs. T. again," Dad said. "What else it means I'm not quite sure."

After supper, Dad and I walked over to Jenny's house to talk to Cathy.

"Maybe she's gone back to a life of crime," Cathy said. "I wonder if she was behind that bank hold-up all along."

"I'm not sure," Dad said. "In her own peculiar way, she was a good person. Certainly she misled us about her past, and she was somewhat confused about property rights. On the other hand, there was always a grain of truth and sense in everything she said and did. She was a formidable opponent in a debate. I think she was a believer in spite of her painful experiences with the Reverend. Childhood influences remain with us a lot longer than we sometimes think. Perhaps that's what she means about old habits being hard to break."

"You think she's joined a religious community?" Cathy said. "I can't see it myself."

"We may never know the answer," Dad said, "but it's going to be very difficult getting along without Mrs. T."

It was more difficult than we thought because Timmy was heartbroken. He said he wouldn't eat another bite of food until Mrs. T. came back. But Dad made bacon, lettuce and tomato sandwiches and as soon as he smelled the bacon cooking, Timmy changed his mind.

Then he nagged us to put an advertisement in all the papers begging Mrs. T. to come back because he couldn't live without her. He badgered Dad so long that finally Dad did put a notice in two papers saying that the Fremedon family was eager to contact their recent caregiver, Mrs. Trowbridge. They would like to hear from her, or from anyone who had information concerning her where- abouts.

"We should offer a big reward for finding her," Timmy said, but eventually he got used to the idea that we'd never see Mrs. T. again.

"She might have changed her name," I said. "People are always doing that."

"She was a riddle, wrapped in a mystery, inside an enigma," Mum said.

"Most people are," Dad said.

JOAN GIVNER is an author and book reviewer who has written a dozen books of biography, auto-biography and fiction, including *Katherine Anne Porter: A Life* and the novels *Half Known Lives* and *Playing Sarah Bernhardt.* The enormously popular *Ellen Fremedon* was her first book for young readers. Joan is a former university professor who now lives on Vancouver Island, where she is working on a third book about Ellen and the eccentric denizens of Partridge Cove.